"We're friends, Nora. Let me be there for you while I'm here."

Her eyes widened as she licked her lips. Desire twisted in Eli's stomach that had nothing to do with the old feelings he had for her. Those were gone, those were a lifetime ago.

This thread of attraction was for the woman she was now, the stubborn, sexy, vibrant woman who kept insisting she didn't need anybody.

"I have friends, Eli." She offered an innocent, sweet smile that didn't quite reach her eyes. "You're here to take care of your father and work. There's no need for you to add anything else to the mix."

Unable to help himself, Eli reached out, slid a hand across her silky cheek and stroked his thumb across her lower lip.

"Maybe I want to add you to the mix," he murmured as he stepped closer.

* * *

THE ST. JOHNS OF STONEROCK:
Three rebellious brothers come home to stay.

Dear Reader,

Welcome to my Harlequin Special Edition debut! I'm so excited to introduce you to the St. Johns of Stonerock. My heroes weren't always upstanding citizens of the small, quaint town. As you'll soon find out, these three brothers who were once hellions have become quite the powerful males: Eli the doctor, Drake the fire chief and Cameron the police chief.

In *Dr. Daddy's Perfect Christmas,* you'll meet ex-soldier turned big-city doctor Eli St. John. He's filling in as the hometown doc and is instantly swept back into the life of his onetime love, Nora Parker... who happens to be widowed and expecting a baby.

Reunion stories have always been a favorite of mine. With any good reunion comes that period of getting to know each other all over again. What Nora and Eli rediscover about each other, and about themselves, will have them fighting for everything they thought they'd lost.

Second chances don't always happen in life. I'm thrilled I could give Eli and Nora their much deserved happily ever after. :)

I hope you enjoy Eli's story and eagerly await the rest of the St. John boys!

Happy reading!

Jules Bennett

Dr. Daddy's
Perfect Christmas

—

Jules Bennett

HARLEQUIN® SPECIAL EDITION®

Recycling programs
for this product may
not exist in your area.

ISBN-13: 978-0-373-65852-7

Dr. Daddy's Perfect Christmas

Copyright © 2014 by Jules Bennett

Printed in U.S.A.

Books by Jules Bennett

Harlequin Special Edition

ΔDr. Daddy's Perfect Christmas #2370

Harlequin Desire

Her Innocence, His Conquest #2081
Caught in the Spotlight #2148
Whatever the Price #2181
Behind Palace Doors #2219
Hollywood House Call #2237
To Tame a Cowboy #2264
Snowbound with a Billionaire #2283
*When Opposites Attract... #2316
*Single Man Meets Single Mom #2325

Silhouette Desire

Seducing the Enemy's Daughter #2004
For Business...or Marriage? #2010
From Boardroom to Wedding Bed? #2046

*The Barrington Trilogy
ΔThe St. Johns of Stonerock

  Other titles by this author available in ebook format.

JULES BENNETT

National bestselling author Jules Bennett's love of story-telling started when she would get in trouble as a child and would tell her parents her imaginary friends were to blame. Since then, her vivid imagination has taken her down a path she'd only dreamed of. And after twelve years of owning and working in salons, she hung up her shears to write full-time.

Jules doesn't just write Happily Ever After—she lives it. Married to her high school sweetheart, Jules and her hubby have two little girls who keep them smiling. She loves to hear from readers! Contact her at authorjules@gmail.com, visit her website, www.julesbennett.com, where you can sign up for her newsletter, or send her a letter at P.O. Box 396, Minford, OH 45653. You can also follow her on Twitter and join her Facebook fan page.

To Stacy Boyd and Gail Chasan,
editorial dream team. Thank you both so much
for loving this series as much as I do!

Chapter One

Don't look, just keep walking.

Dr. Eli St. John walked up the freshly dusted, snow-covered sidewalk toward his parents' bungalow and refused to even glance over to their neighbor's house.

Since he'd be calling Stonerock, Tennessee, home again for the next few months, he'd no doubt see that neighbor more often than he'd like. But on his first day back, he preferred to ease into being home, ease into knowing she was now within reaching distance. Not that he would do anything about it.

He was such a coward.

An uncomfortable weight settled in his chest at the thought of seeing his one-time love, the woman he'd never forgotten, the woman who'd married his best friend.

Eli wiped the snow off the bottom of his boots on a Santa Claus welcome mat, and before he could reach for the handle, the door swung wide open, causing an evergreen Christmas wreath to bounce in protest.

"I'm so glad you're here. I knew we could count on you."

Eli sank into his mother's familiar embrace. Before he could step over the threshold of the front door, his mother, Bev, was there to greet him with a smile and love. Just like she'd done each time he'd come home from a tour of duty.

Now, the times he had sneaked in after curfew as a teen were a different story. But that hell-raiser had grown up, leaving the proverbial good times behind.

Leaving Nora Parker behind. Now that he was going to be home for a good bit of time, dodging the one woman who still owned a small portion of his heart would be nearly impossible. Not only was she his parents' neighbor, she was a recent widow, and his parents loved her like she was the daughter they never had.

Turning his attention back to the reason for his homecoming, Eli eased back from his mother's embrace and met her gaze.

"What's this?" she asked, brushing her fingertip along his most recent scar.

Refusing to get into the reasons behind the scar, he shrugged. "Army injury."

He wasn't lying, technically. There was no way he would ever come clean about the ugly reminder of how he'd spent his last encounter with his best friend.

The last time he'd seen Todd alive, they'd gotten into a drunken fistfight. Out of character for both of them, but Eli would do it again in a heartbeat, given the reasons behind the unleashed rage.

His mother hugged him again. "I'm so proud of you for serving, but selfishly I'm glad you're done for good."

Bev pulled back and Eli stepped into the foyer. "How's Dad?"

Nodding, she started forward toward the living room. "He's okay. You of all people know doctors make the worst patients."

Eli laughed, thankful that he was home, but worried what he'd encounter when he saw his father. The man had always been so robust, so full of life and busy caring for others. But his father had failed a stress test earlier in the week and a heart cath showed he had some major blockage.

Eli had been a medic in the army the past several years, but since he got out six months ago, he'd been an ER doctor in Atlanta, and he'd seen his fair share of massive heart attacks. Chest pain was nothing to mess around with. Since his father hadn't been having pain, they scheduled the surgery for tomorrow, for which Eli was thankful. The drive on his way up from Georgia had given him enough time to prepare himself.

And enough time to work on scenarios and re-actions to seeing Nora. Why did he care? Shouldn't time and distance have severed any ties he had to her? They were different people now and whatever feelings they'd had in the past were left there when he chose to walk away from her.

Hardest decision of his life, to leave her and go fight for his country.

The scar on his face proved he'd never fully gotten over her, even though they'd both moved on.

They'd each made their choices, and there was no going back.

Eli tried to slide those thoughts from his mind as he followed his mother toward the living room. He was here for his father first and foremost…not to re-hash or run from emotions he'd felt years ago. He had his own life now, one he loved and was eager to get back to once his father was cleared to return to work.

Eli had seen countless patients laid up, recover-ing or even dying, but when your father was the one being treated, the whole scenario changed. Eli wasn't a fan of being back home for a long period of time, but there was no way he'd leave his father or his fa-ther's patients in a bind.

Fortunately, Eli had handled seventeen years in the military and in medical school so coming home to a disgruntled father, who was waiting on quadruple bypass surgery instead of practicing medicine him-self, was nothing Eli couldn't handle.

Eli moved through the old bungalow-style home, leaving his suitcase in the foyer. As much as he loved coming home for visits, he'd never done so with the intention of staying longer than a few days. And in those visits home, he'd managed to avoid Nora for the most part. He'd seen her and even exchanged the requisite pleasantries, but other than that, he'd kept his distance.

Now he'd be home—at a minimum—for the rest of the winter and into the spring.

Nothing like being thirty-five years old and living with Mommy and Daddy again. Of course he'd do anything for his parents, including give up his bachelor lifestyle. Family had always come first, no matter what. At least he was going to be staying in the apartment above the garage. That was still somewhat private.

Eli stepped into the living room where his father was reclined in the old, plush chair that should've been retired to a garbage dump about five years ago. The man was a doctor; he could afford new furniture, for heaven's sake.

Familiar ornaments adorned the full artificial tree that occupied the corner of the space. His mother still hung all of their stockings along the edge of the mantel even though Eli and his brothers had each moved out right after they graduated. The worn-in comfort of the home, especially now at Christmas, helped ease his nerves in dealing with the inevitable reunion with Nora. He wasn't so worried about the old feelings creeping up; he was more worried about how he could look her in the eye when he knew a truth she could never uncover.

Eli glanced from the television to his father. Remote in one hand, Dr. Mac St. John gave the television the one-fingered salute with the other.

Suppressing a chuckle, Eli stepped closer, but he

knew what he'd find on the TV—sports. His father had always been a sports fanatic, namely football. Apparently this game was not to his liking. Or, more to the point, the refs' decisions weren't to his liking.

"Still disagreeing with their calls?" Eli asked.

His dad turned to face him and in one swift motion Mac had the footrest down and was on his feet. "Well, there's one of my boys."

Mac wrapped his arms around Eli's shoulders and gave him a manly slap on the back. Eli returned his father's embrace, welcoming the comforting touch. At one time Eli and his brothers feared the wrath of their father, but Eli now understood that the anger from his dad had only stemmed from fear and love. Eli didn't even want to think about what he and his brothers had put their parents through.

His mother had once said that raising teenagers wasn't for wimps. At the rate Eli was going with his career really taking root, he didn't have time to date, let alone find a wife and have children. Besides, he'd settled pretty well into his bachelor status. Working in Atlanta with a promotion on the horizon was the main component in his life, other than his parents and brothers.

"Let me look at you." His father eased back down into his chair, resting his hands on his knees. "You look good, son. Real good. You don't know how much this means to me that you're willing to fill in."

Eli didn't want to think about the patients at his dad's office. More than likely they were the same judgmental people who lived here when he was a havoc-wreaking teen. He and his brothers hadn't exactly been the town's golden boys.

Apparently stealing street signs, racing down Main Street in dual-exhaust trucks and spray painting old buildings was frowned upon. Not that anyone could prove the St. John boys had anything to do with such shenanigans. Eli and his brothers were way too sneaky and smart to get caught.

On a sigh, Eli shook away the memories. People in small towns never forgot the person you used to be. Even worse, they never let *you* forget it, either. Yeah, he'd be well received as the new hometown doctor.

Eventually they'd see he had changed, but whether they did or didn't, he was heading back to Atlanta in—hopefully—three months. Eli was already anxious to get back.

The head of the trauma unit was going to retire in a couple of months. An old army buddy had given Eli the heads-up that the position was coming available. Eli had actually only worked in the ER for a few months, but since he was already an internal doctor, he had a leg up on any outsiders vying for the position.

He couldn't worry about that right now, but he was hopeful that he would hear something soon.

"What time is your surgery scheduled in the morning?" Eli asked, taking a seat next to his mother on the old floral sofa that belonged in the same Dumpster as the recliner.

"They're doing it at seven," she told him. "But

they're going to admit him this evening. We wanted to wait until you came before we left."

Eli glanced to his watch, then over to his dad. "Are you ready to go or do we need to finish this game you're cursing under your breath about?"

His father pointed the remote at the TV, shutting it off. "I guess we can go. Let it be known that I am not happy about having my independence taken away."

Eli laughed. "Noted. Let it also be known we're glad you're having surgery so you'll be around for a few more years."

The doorbell chimed through the house and Eli held up his hand. "I'll get it. You two go get whatever you need to take to the hospital."

He figured his parents were already very well prepared to go. He also knew as the hometown doctor his father was popular and figured whoever was at the door was here to send Mac off. Eli thought it best to intercept the visitor and usher his parents on out the door before throngs of people came by.

Eli neglected to glance out the sidelights before he jerked the door open to the one woman who could make his knees weak and his gut clench.

All that rehearsing in the car did absolutely no good when he was rendered speechless.

Nora Parker, the epitome of hometown girl, stood on his parents' porch looking all bright and fresh even as the blistery cold winds swirled about. She'd wrapped herself in a cheerful red coat and multi-striped hat and matching scarf.

The girl who had won over the hearts of his parents

when his youngest brother, Drake, had befriended her in junior high and brought her home after school still had a place in their lives. Shortly thereafter she'd stolen his heart and just a few years later they'd turned their backs on each other, him to pursue his dreams, her to make a life in the only place she wanted to call home.

Now, here she was, no doubt checking in on his father. Their inevitable time together was about to begin whether he was mentally prepared for it or not.

Game on.

"Eli." With eyes wide, she pasted on a radiant smile. "I knew you were coming home, but I didn't expect to see you here tonight. I didn't miss Mac and Bev, did I?"

Eli forced himself to snap out of this stupefied state and stop staring like some lustful teen. Good grief, he hadn't even invited her in from the biting cold.

"You didn't miss them. Come on in." He gestured, opening the door wider. "It's freezing out there."

Her sweet, floral perfume slid right under his nose as she passed through. Eli closed the door, turning to offer to take her coat, but, like an idiot, he became mesmerized as she started talking.

For pity's sake, he acted like he'd never seen a female before. This wasn't just any female. This was the one girl who'd stolen his not-so-innocent heart at the age of sixteen. This was the girl who had finally settled down four years ago with his best friend.

This was the girl who had no idea about the deceit behind her own marriage and the lies behind her late husband. Eli couldn't tell her, though. He'd never purposely hurt Nora again. Once was enough to leave him scarred. Literally.

"So," she said, looking around. "They're still here?"

Oh, right. While he was fighting the urge to travel down that lane of not-so-pleasant memories, she'd been waiting for a response.

"We were just getting ready to go," he supplied. "Come on into the living room. Do you need me to take your coat?"

"Oh, no. I can't stay long."

He followed her, clutching his fists the whole way. Those instant lustful feelings that had slammed into him at the sight of her standing on his parents' porch had better just go away. How disrespectful could he be? A giant gap of years lived between them, proving nothing from the past was the same.

Eli, Nora and her late husband, Todd, had gone to the same school, grown up in this same small town. Not only that, Eli had served alongside Todd in the army up until six months earlier when Eli had gotten out for good, but Todd had reenlisted…and only a few months ago he'd been killed in action.

"I'm sorry about Todd," he told her as she stood in the foyer. "I wasn't able to get back for the funeral due to my work schedule, but I was thinking about you."

Wasn't that the story of his life? He'd thought about her too much over the years. But they'd made the mutual decision to sever their relationship and he couldn't fault her for moving on, marrying and having a life. Even if that life had been a lie and she had no clue.

At the age of eighteen, he'd been confident and cocky that he could make the world a better place and had thought for sure Nora would come with him and share his dream. But she'd had strong reasons for wanting to stay, just as he had strong reasons for leaving. So they'd been at a stalemate, both too young and stubborn to budge, thinking love would get them through.

Nora's misty eyes held his. "Thanks. It's been… rough, but I'm doing okay."

Eli noticed the second she zeroed in on the scar running from just above his brow, down and into his hairline close to his ear. She started to reach up and Eli froze, steeling himself for her touch. When her hand dropped before she could make contact, he blew out a breath.

Eli wasn't offering an explanation, and if she asked, he'd have to be vague. That scar mocked him each day in the mirror, reminding him of the secret he still kept for a dead man.

An awkward silence settled between them, but thankfully his mother came into the room, breaking the tension. Since when didn't he know how to handle a woman?

Nora wasn't just any woman, though. She was special. Trying to start anything with her now, after all this time, would just be wrong. With her a recent widow and him leaving in a few months…yeah, not a good idea. So, he'd just have to put his emotions in check and do the job he came here to do.

Besides, so much time had passed; they were nowhere near the same people.

"Nora," his mother greeted with open arms, and the two women embraced each other. "Is everything okay?"

"Everything is fine." Nora eased back. "I just wanted to let you know that I'll stop by the hospital to bring some lunch after work tomorrow. I know the surgery can take several hours."

Eli stood by the door, still watching this interaction between his high school sweetheart and his mother. It was like time had stood still, only it hadn't. Time had been cruel and had taken each of them down different paths, paths that led to heartache and deceit. Paths that led in totally opposite directions and as far apart as two people once in love could get.

And yet here they were, full circle. Eli wanted to reach out, even hug her in a friendly gesture. He'd lost that right years ago and had no one to blame but himself.

Already the ache in seeing her had settled deep in his chest. They were only on day one so how in the hell did he expect to see her nearly every day? Because he knew full well that Nora loved Mac and Bev as much as he did and she'd be around checking on them, worried about them.

Looked like he was about to pay his penance for leaving her behind.

Oh, sweet mercy. This inescapable, awkward reunion smacked her in the face and left her utterly speechless. Remaining friends with Eli's family had once been torture when Eli had first enlisted. She adored Mac and Bev so much that even when he broke things off and joined the army, she still held on to that precious bond with his parents. They were truly the closest thing to having her own and the teen in her embraced the stability.

Nora tried, she really did, to focus on what Bev was saying, but her mind was on the man who stood just over her shoulder. The man she'd once thought to be "the one." The man who had told her over and over that when he graduated he planned on enlisting to explore and change the world. It wasn't the fact he was enlisting that broke them. She was proud of him for wanting to fight for freedoms. The issue was that Eli never had any intention of returning and settling down in this small town.

At one time, naively, she'd thought he'd miss her so bad he'd come crawling back. Yeah, she'd held that much hope in their relationship. When he'd been gone for enough time she knew there was no chance, she cut her losses and started dating Todd. She'd been moved around so much as a kid, she simply longed for a home and some stability. Things she thought Todd could offer.

Eli's fresh, masculine aroma had surrounded her when she'd passed by him in the foyer. There was no way she was letting him help her with her coat because she couldn't stay long…and she had another reason to hide behind the heavy wool.

After the shock of seeing Eli—with a fresh-looking, jagged facial scar—faded, her mind instantly went to their high school days when he'd try anything to get her to cross the "good girl" line. But as soon as that memory hit her, her mind drifted to Todd. She'd been doing so well lately with keeping her emotions in check. Maybe they hadn't had the best or most ideal marriage, but she mourned the man who sacrificed himself for his country.

In all honesty Eli had probably spent more time with Todd than Nora had because the two had been deployed months upon months together in Iraq over the past four years. Best friends in school turned army buddies living through some of the harshest conditions.

She'd thought when she'd married Todd that he would get out of the army, but he'd decided to stay. After four years of marriage, most of them spent with him deployed, Nora had finally lost her husband for good.

Now, due to the financial strain of living on one income, she might have to sell her home. The death benefits and pension weren't going near as far as she'd hoped.

Nora blinked back tears that were so easy to flow. Seeing Eli conjured up that part of her mind she associated with Todd and Eli together. The two men she'd loved. The two men she'd lost. She wanted to be angry at both of them for leaving her, but what good would that do?

While she knew she'd run into Eli over the next day or so, she hadn't planned on it being after a grueling day at the clinic. Between multiple cases of worms, kennel cough and vaccinations, she was ready to prop her feet up and dig into a big bowl of Rocky Road ice cream for dinner and snuggle with her finicky cat, Kerfluffle.

Most people probably wanted hot soup on a cold day like today, but she wanted the good stuff. The fattening stuff. It's not like her expanding waistline would suffer any more than it already had. Nora knew she smelled like dog and was covered in fur— occupational hazard—but she hadn't expected to see Eli before she could at least shower, change from her scrubs and attempt to fix her hair...and a half-falling ponytail did not count as fixed.

Not that she was trying to get his attention, but she at least wanted to look somewhat put together and not like a bag lady.

A pregnant bag lady. This was one time in her life she was thankful for her height. At least the weight could spread out more and her belly barely had a bump. Eli didn't know she was pregnant, as far as she knew, and it really wasn't a topic she wanted to broach with him. While she embraced the love of her small town and the folks who'd rallied around her upon Todd's death and her pregnancy discovery all within days of each other, the last thing she wanted was to see pity in Eli's eyes.

She'd seen that look years ago when they'd broken things off and she hoped to God she never had to see it again.

"If you don't mind," Bev said.

Nora blinked and smiled. "I'm sorry. What?"

Bev patted her arm, offering a wide grin. "You're exhausted, honey. Go home and put your feet up."

"No, no. I'm fine. My mind wandered and I didn't hear what you said."

Wandered, took a hard right and ended up in la-la land. Such was the story of her life. Always daydreaming, because reality was starting to flat-out suck.

Except for the precious baby she carried. No way could Nora be upset about something so miraculous—no matter the circumstances.

"I just said it would be wonderful if you could bring lunch for us tomorrow if you didn't mind," Bev said, still holding on to Nora's arm. "But only if you're already coming down. Don't make a special trip."

"Oh, no. I don't mind at all."

Eli shuffled his feet behind her and Nora turned to see his eyes directly locked on to hers. No matter how hard she tried she couldn't block old memories from sliding into the forefront of her mind.

Her mother may have been a drifter, but one of her boyfriends that had come and gone had lived in Stonerock. When Nora had been a teen they'd moved here and Nora knew this was the place she'd stay. Her mother had hung around for a few years, allowing Nora to actually make friends, find teen love and experience her first heartache.

Speaking of, Eli now held her gaze with those

dark-as-sin eyes that used to mesmerize her. They still did.

"Bringing lunch would mean a lot to us, Nora," he told her.

Why did she have to still find him attractive? Why did that new scar intrigue her and make her want to know all about his life since he'd left?

Stupid hormones. She did not have time for this.

"There's my girl."

Nora turned to see Mac coming down the hall, a huge smile on his face and arms open wide. She loved this family, she honestly did, and they'd cared for her for so long she didn't know what she'd do without them.

They'd been there for her when Eli had gone off to the army and her mother had moved on. Mac had actually helped her with vet school, covering what financial aid hadn't.

They'd been there when Todd was killed. Mac and Bev were the loving, doting parents she'd always longed for.

And the thought of Mac having open-heart surgery terrified her. She knew he needed it, but there was always that chance that something could go wrong. Even though she treated animals, she knew more than enough about the surgery to be worried.

"Oh, now." Mac took her into his arms and patted her. "Don't tear up on me, Nora. I'll be fine and back home grumbling in no time."

Nora sniffed and eased back in Mac's arms. "I'm just tired, that's all. I know you'll be in good hands and I'll be there to make sure your family is taken care of."

Mac squeezed her shoulders and nodded. "I couldn't ask for a better daughter."

Nora's heart squeezed. He'd often referred to her as the daughter he'd never had. Being friends with Eli's younger brother Drake had introduced her to the family, but it wasn't until she started dating Eli that she truly felt the family bond she'd always craved. She'd thought watching him leave was the hardest thing she'd ever face. Boy was she wrong. The past few years had been difficult, but the past several months had been a whole new level of hell. One day at a time she was crawling out, trying to get back to some sort of stability in her life before she brought a baby into this world.

"I better let you guys go." Nora moved toward the door, careful not to touch Eli. "I'll be praying for you, Mac, and I'll be by the hospital after work."

She fled the family scene before she really did something stupid like break down in full snot-and-tears mode. Who knew pregnancies could produce such a juxtaposition of emotions?

Heading to her home next door, Nora crossed the lawn, speckled with a hint of snowflakes. She knew there was no way just one pint of Rocky Road would soothe her tonight and wine was out of the question.

There was only one thing left to do: she'd have to pull out all the stops and liberate the large supreme pizza from her freezer emergency stash. And seeing Eli looking all perfectly intriguing and mysterious with his scar and demanding presence definitely constituted an emergency.

While she hated pity from others, Nora felt she was entitled to throw herself a pity party. Once she gorged herself on junk and maybe indulged in a bubble bath, she'd feel better.

She placed a hand on her bump and smiled. She had four months to regain control of her life and emotions because, no matter the turmoil, Nora would provide stability and love to this baby…even if she was alone.

Chapter Two

The surgery went beautifully and there were no complications.

Eli breathed a sigh of relief once the cardiologist confirmed the news. He also told them Mac would need to be monitored for a few hours before he could have visitors.

"Now we have to focus on getting him better and making sure he takes care of himself," Cameron said, taking a seat back in the waiting area.

Eli nodded to his younger brother. "I agree. And doctors are such a pain to treat."

Drake laughed, plopping right next to Eli. "Are you the pot or the kettle, Dr. St. John?"

"Boys," Bev scolded. "I will make sure your father watches what he eats and gets more exercise."

"Lifting the remote in his off time does not constitute as a workout," Eli told her, reaching across to squeeze her hand. "But if I know Dad, this scared him. He may not admit it, but he'll start being more cautious."

A cell phone chimed and Eli jerked around to see both Cameron and Drake checking their sides. As the police captain, Cameron tended to be popular even off his shift, and as the local fire chief, Drake was always in demand, too.

Yeah, these rebel teens did all right for themselves, despite what the townsfolk may have initially thought.

Cameron came to his feet. "I'm the winner. Be right back."

He walked through the double doors and headed out, taking his cell from his pocket. Eli was a minority in that he loved being on call. He'd been home less than twenty-four hours, but he already missed being needed, missed saving people under high-pressure circumstances.

And for the next three months, he'd be right here in Stonerock, Tennessee, treating cold and flu symptoms, random viruses and allergies, if spring hit early.

"Sorry I'm late."

Eli glanced up to see Nora breezing in. She had on that happy gear again with the bright red coat, colorful scarf and hat. Juggling sacks of food and another sack full of bottles of water, she looked very rushed and worn as tendrils of wispy blond hair slid from her cap.

Both he and Drake came to their feet to help her.

"I had to fit in a last-minute emergency." She handed over the drinks and food and collapsed into the nearest seat. "Have you heard anything?"

"The doctor just came out and said he did beautifully," Bev said, taking a bottle of water from Drake.

Nora's shoulders relaxed, her head tilted back against the chair and she sighed. "That's such a relief. How are you all holding up? I saw Cameron out front on the phone."

"We're doing great now that Dad is out of surgery and food arrived," Drake told her with a slight wink.

Eli didn't want his youngest brother winking at Nora. The two may be old friends, but Eli was, well, he was…absolutely nothing in her life. So if Drake wanted to wink, then so be it. That didn't mean Eli had to like it or watch.

Nora had to be exhausted because she sat stone-still, wearing her coat and hat. Apparently she wasn't staying.

Eli unwrapped a burger and tore into it, focusing on his growling stomach and not the dark circles beneath Nora's eyes or the way her face had slimmed down since he'd seen her the last time he'd visited.

The woman looked physically drained and it would be completely rude of him to say anything. Besides, he had no place in her personal life. Perhaps working herself like mad was her only way of coping with Todd's death.

And even though Todd had died a hero to his country, the man didn't deserve Nora's tears…or Eli's heavy dose of remorse.

"How are you feeling?" Bev asked Nora.

Nora lifted her lids and turned to smile at his mother. "I'm just tired. Thankfully the weekend is here and I have the next two days off. That is unless someone needs me, in which case they'll call me at home or just come knocking on my door, pet carrier in hand."

"You should consider hiring someone else to help you or getting stricter on your hours," Bev offered.

Nora shook her head. "I'm going to have to pretty soon. I have a couple of people in mind. It will all depend on what they will accept for payment."

Eli listened, but refused to get involved. Over and over he kept telling himself he was only here for a short time. Whatever was going on now would still be going on long after he was gone.

Five years ago, when he'd considered coming back, he'd discovered Nora and Todd had started dating. Eli knew then he'd blown his chance for a reunion. Now Eli needed to stay focused on his own goals of helping his father by working in his clinic and getting back to the potential new job when he returned to Atlanta. End of story. He wasn't back here to do anything but to be a fill-in…and not for a late husband.

"The doctor said we could go back and see Mac, but not until later," Bev said, pushing her silver hair behind her ears. "Why don't you guys take a break and come back this evening."

Cameron came striding down the hallway, sliding his cell back into the pocket of his jeans. He leaned down, placed a very innocent peck on Nora's cheek, and Eli had to take another bite of his burger to keep from reacting.

This was a widow, for crying out loud. Not only did his brothers have no room to wink or give kisses, he sure as hell had no business getting jealous.

"Thanks for the food," Cameron said, grabbing the last burger. "You're an angel."

"Your standards are low if you're that impressed over a cheeseburger."

The banter between his brothers and Nora took Eli back to when they were all teens, before life intervened…before he'd grown strong feelings for her and watched her marry another man.

She'd fit into his family beautifully. Everyone had thought he and Nora would end up together. Their ultimate dreams and the bigger picture just didn't match up. But that didn't mean he'd ever stopped caring for her…or loving her.

"I'm going to head to the clinic and check things out." Eli came to his feet and tossed his trash in the wastebasket beside his chair. "I'd like to glance at the schedule for next week and look at some charts."

"Don't mess too much up in the office area," Drake warned. "If you do, Lulu will have your head."

Eli groaned. His father's receptionist, real name unknown, was not a typical receptionist. In fact, she was flat-out weird and if she hadn't been at his dad's office for the past twenty years, he'd suggest his father hire someone else. But she knew the place inside and out and could answer any questions he had.

Eli only hoped she'd keep the flask at home, the

nail files put away and her cleavage covered while she assisted him for the next few months.

"I promise not to bother any of Lulu's things," he stated.

Bev stood, wrapped her arms around him and kissed his cheek. "You don't know what it means that you're here, Eli."

Easing back, Eli looked her in the eye and smiled. "I wouldn't be anywhere else, Mom."

After making sure one of his brothers would be there for their mom until he returned, he said a quick goodbye to Nora, who had also come to her feet.

"I'll walk out with you," she said. "If that's okay."

Eli nodded. This was going to be a long three months if he didn't get over these emotions that kept sliding up and choking him. He'd managed to dodge such strong feelings before when he'd visit because the occasional "hi" as they passed in the yard didn't resurrect too much. The thought of spending actual time with her, probably learning more about her personal life, had Eli's mind all in a jumbled mess.

Nora walked by his side toward the double sliding glass doors leading outside. They'd passed the concrete fountain in the middle of the circular drive-up area and visitor benches before she finally broke the uncomfortable silence.

"You don't seem happy to be back."

Eli squinted against the afternoon sun glistening off the light dusting of snow on the grass and guided her down the sidewalk toward the visitor parking. "I've been nervous with Dad's surgery. And to be honest, I'm anxious about his practice. I hope the people in town will accept me as their doctor while dad's recovering."

Nora's delicate hand came up to his forearm as she stopped walking. Eli turned to look at her. The unusually bright winter sun almost created a halo effect around her colorful hat. When he noticed her squinting against the sun, too, Eli shifted his stance to cast a shadow over her.

"What I meant to say was, you seem uneasy with me," she said, holding his gaze as if she dared him to look away.

Inwardly he smiled. He'd forgotten how she'd always been a take-charge type, never one to back down even if a topic was uncomfortable or awkward.

"I am," he told her honestly. "I didn't get to make it back for Todd's funeral and I'm not quite sure what to say to you now that I'm here."

Okay, that wasn't a total lie, but it was just another layer to his unsettled mood.

Her hand slid from his as she pulled her coat tighter over her chest, crossing her arms. The slight breeze picked up strands of her low ponytail and sent pieces dancing around her shoulder.

"You don't have to say anything, Eli. No words will bring him back and I won't fall apart if you mention his name. He died doing what he loved, but I'm getting along." She offered a tender smile. "You and I used to be so close."

She inched closer, still holding his eyes with her own. Eli swallowed, but held her gaze. Nothing could make him turn away from such beauty. She'd always been able to captivate him with no effort on her part.

"All I need right now are friends," she told him, her bright blue eyes searching his. "Can you handle that?"

Could he handle being her friend? He could, but there would be that secret silently settling between them, forming an invisible wedge.

Her pleading eyes tugged at his heart and he couldn't deny her.

"I can handle that," he told her with a brief nod.

She cupped her gloved hand over his cheek and the warmth spread throughout him. "I'm glad you're back, even if it is for a short time." She flashed him a knockout smile, then dropped her hand and pulled her coat back around her as if to shield herself against the chilly breeze.

Nora may act like everything was fine, but Eli's body was still reeling from her innocent touch. Everything about her gesture had been harmless. And yet he could still feel her softness as her hand slid against his cheek—even though he hadn't felt her bare skin.

"I'm so relieved the surgery was a success," she told him, turning to walk again. "I've been a nervous wreck since we found out he'd have to have it."

Eli kept his pace slow so she could remain by his side and in case there was a skiff of snow on the walk. He didn't mind the cold; he would've walked anywhere she wanted to go if she'd just keep talking to him. He'd missed spending time with her. Because even though they'd parted ways, she'd always been so easy to talk to, so understanding and compassionate.

They'd been best friends at one time and he'd yet to find anyone else he shared such a strong bond with outside of his family.

"I honestly was, too," Eli told her. "I knew he was in good hands here, but you never know when something can go wrong."

"How did you manage to get off work for so long?" she asked, stopping beside a small silver SUV. "That wasn't much notice considering they told him yesterday he'd be having surgery."

"I requested an emergency FMLA." When she gave him a questioning look he clarified. "A family leave of absence. It's for twelve weeks. If Dad is better before then, I can return, but that's the limit I can be gone."

"You like it in Atlanta?" she asked.

"I love Atlanta," he told her without hesitation. "Even though I just settled in a few months ago, I love the hospital, the staff. I love the city itself."

A slight smile tipped one corner of her mouth. "You were always so eager to leave."

Yeah, he'd had it all figured out. First graduation, then the army, then seeing the world.

But his plans got a bit derailed and he'd gone back into the army before getting out and looking for a job in his field.

So far, he'd accomplished every career goal he'd ever wanted. But what about his personal life? What goals had he worked toward or even set for himself outside of his career?

"I'm not a small-town guy," he told her. "I knew when I left I wanted something more."

This topic was starting to venture into a territory he truly didn't think either of them was ready for so he nodded toward the car he'd seen in her drive. "This you?"

"Yeah. I may be back later, but right now I need to go home and lie down."

Not for the first time he noticed she was a bit pale, which only showcased those dark circles beneath her eyes even more.

"Are you feeling okay?"

She sighed and nodded. "Yeah, just tired a lot lately."

"You're working too hard, then."

Nora shrugged without defending herself as most people would do. "If I don't see you back here, I'll see you at your parents' house."

"Thanks for being there for them," he told her, holding the door open for her. "Over the years when I've been overseas, you've just…you've always been there and I'm not sure I ever said thank you."

Nora's eyes misted as she met his gaze overtop the car door. "I love your parents, Eli. Just because we stopped dating didn't mean I loved or cared for them any less. I'm happy we have one another because, trust me, they've been there for me, too."

She turned and got behind the wheel before he could question her. His mother and father rarely mentioned Nora other than in occasional conversations and then when Todd had passed. They'd never talked about her needing them or hard times. He assumed they didn't mention it because they knew he had moved on.

Nora's sad smile told him her life had been anything but what she'd envisioned. She was hiding something and as bad as he wanted to know what that was, he knew he had no place in her life...past or present.

Chapter Three

Nora was pretty much hugging the toilet. Not her most shining moment in life, but she had no control of certain bodily functions lately.

The second she'd opened that bathroom cleaner her stomach had revolted and all she knew was that she was thankful she'd already been in the bathroom because there was no holding it back.

Wasn't morning sickness supposed to be in the morning and in the first trimester? Come on, life, could she get some slack cut here?

At twenty weeks' pregnant her ob-gyn had assured her that the nausea, exhaustion and sickness were quite normal and every pregnancy was different so Nora couldn't compare all her experiences to things she'd seen online.

The exhaustion she could handle, but the nausea that chose to hit her at random times during the day really left her helpless. Talk about awkward when she was doing an exam on an animal. So far she'd only had to leave the room twice and thankfully her clients were understanding.

Nora eased back, praying this round was over. Apparently the bathroom wasn't going to get cleaned, not by her, anyway. She was flat-out drained and, as of this moment, didn't even have the energy to stand, let alone scrub.

Mac was coming home today and she'd wanted to surprise them with a nice, clean house. There was no way Bev would have the time to clean with taking care of Mac. It wasn't much, but she felt like she should do something to help them.

She also had made up a few casseroles and put them in the deep freezer in the garage so hopefully Bev wouldn't have to worry about cooking for a while.

Nora had just reached and flushed the commode when she heard the front door close. Perking an ear, because that's all she had the energy to perk right now, she listened for voices, but didn't hear any. At least it wasn't Bev and Mac.

Heavy footsteps stopped right outside the bathroom door and Nora glanced over her shoulder. Her eyes traveled up denim-clad legs, a dark gray wool coat, and landed on the most handsome face peeking from beneath a black knit cap. Dark stubble covered his jawline, and between that ruggedness and the scar peeking out of the hat, he looked even more intriguing and attractive than ever.

Eli leaned against the doorway and crossed his arms over his chest. Seeing as how she'd been cleaning, she'd left the door open to let out some of the chemical smell.

He raised a brow. "What are you doing on the floor?"

"Oh, you know, just resting." Nora tried to smile, but she wasn't quite sure she pulled it off. "Sorry. I was trying to help…"

The room was spinning again, but she turned her cheek to rest her face on the cool tile on the wall. She would not pass out. But if she did, at least she was still on the floor and wouldn't have far to go down.

"Nora. Are you okay?"

Eli squatted down, resting a hand against her forehead, instantly turning into a doctor before her. Nora closed her eyes at the feel of his gentle touch, resisting the urge to lean into his strength and draw from it. How many lives had those hands healed? Did he have a clue just how powerless she was right now between her weakened state and his innocent caress?

"I'm just not feeling well," she told him, being as honest as she could. "I wanted to clean before your mom and dad came home."

Eli muttered something under his breath, then sighed. "Can you walk?"

She could barely hold her head up, so standing on her legs and putting one foot in front of the other was out of the question. And if the room didn't quit spinning, she didn't know how much longer she could go without lying down.

"Maybe in a bit."

She lifted her lids and met his concerned gaze. Those dark eyes were always so mesmerizing. Maybe if she just focused on that, on him…

No, she had enough to focus on as it was. A baby, coming to grips with the fact she'd been married to a man who hadn't truly loved her and now left her a pregnant widow, plus the very great possibility she'd have to find a smaller, less expensive house.

Before she knew what Eli had planned, he'd wrapped one arm around her shoulders and slid another arm beneath her knees. He came to his feet with ease and Nora rested her head against his warm shoulder. If she had more strength she'd be embarrassed he'd found her in such a humbling position, but she was too sick to care.

"I'm sorry, Eli."

"Don't be sorry for caring about my parents," he told her, easing sideways down the hallway and then up the stairs. "Be sorry that you're not listening to your body and taking it easy."

She didn't protest when he took her into his old bedroom.

"I'll be fine," she promised. "I just need to lie still for a few minutes until this nausea subsides."

"Have you had a fever?" he asked.

"No."

There was absolutely no way she was going to tell

him about the baby. He would find out soon enough. There were only so many ways she could camouflage her belly. She just wasn't ready to tell him—didn't want to see the pity in his eyes, didn't want him to feel like she was an obligation because they'd been friends and Todd had been his friend, too.

Nora didn't have her coat as a shield today, but the yoga pants and oversize sweatshirt certainly did the trick.

"How about aches?" he asked, gently laying her down on the bed. "This is flu season."

"No. I know it's not the flu."

Nora couldn't help the sigh that escaped her as she sank into the soft, plush comforter. All she could smell was Eli's strong, woodsy cologne and she took a deep breath, wanting to take in as much of him as she could.

Funny, that smell didn't turn her stomach. Obviously that was a sign she should lay off cleaning for the safety of her health.

That was a pregnancy rule she could get behind.

"You don't have a fever," he went on. "Maybe it was just something you ate that didn't agree with you."

Nora glanced up at him and attempted a grin. "Must be. Just give me a minute and I'll finish picking up."

"Like hell you will," he informed her. "I came back from the hospital early to get things ready for Dad. Cameron is there to bring Mom and Dad home when he's released."

"I have casseroles in the freezer in the garage," she told him. "I had already washed the few dishes in the sink and put them away. I dusted and ran the sweeper. All that's left is the bathroom downstairs, which is where I was when I got sick."

Eli held her gaze and she couldn't look away if she tried. Those broad shoulders filled out the dark gray wool coat that he'd yet to take off, but somewhere along the way he'd removed the hat. That dark, messy hair looked as if he'd just stepped out of his lover's bed, and his eyes, still fixed on hers, were so dark they were nearly black.

All three brothers had those eyes, the same as their father's. There was something about Eli's that captivated her, held her. He was the type of man who demanded attention without saying a word. How could she not comply?

"When did you eat last?" he asked, shrugging out of his coat and laying it on the end of the bed.

She thought back to the dry toast she'd choked down with orange juice for breakfast. "About nine."

Eli glanced to his wristwatch and glared at her. "It's nearly three, Nora."

"I really wasn't hungry and I didn't feel that great. I just wanted to clean and get back home."

"No one expected you to tidy up the place. Not to sound ungrateful, I appreciate the gesture and so will Mom, but you have to listen to your body."

Well, right now her body was saying to stay in this cozy bed and let someone wait on her hand and foot.

"I'm listening, Doc." He continued to glare and Nora tapped his very toned, very chiseled biceps. "Smile. I'm fine."

"Your color is coming back."

"See? Told you I just needed to lie down for a bit."

She glanced beyond his shoulder to the photos displayed on his old dresser. A picture of him in Iraq, one of him graduating from medical school, another of him in some type of surgical field. No doubt his mother had proudly put these photos into frames. Just more reminders that he wasn't staying and his life was elsewhere. He'd worked hard to become a prominent doctor and she was so glad he'd not only chased his dream, but he'd captured it with both hands.

"Why am I in your old room?" she asked, bringing her eyes back to his.

"Because I wanted you to lie down."

"What about the couch?"

His eyes roamed over her face, to her mouth and back up. "I thought you might need to rest and you'd be able to do that up here away from the commotion of Mom and Dad coming home in a bit."

Nora started to sit up. "I better put a casserole in the oven. It has to bake for a while."

Eli put his hand on her shoulder and eased her back down. "I can do it, Precious."

She froze. He'd always called her that when they'd dated.

As if realizing what had just slipped out of his mouth, Eli cursed. With his hand still on her shoulder and their faces only inches apart, she trembled. No man had ever affected her the way Eli did.

Not even the man who'd promised to love, honor and be faithful. Her heart clenched from so much emotion. Even though Todd obviously hadn't cared for their marriage, he was the father of this unborn baby and he didn't deserve to die.

"Relax," Eli whispered. "When was the last time someone looked out for you?"

Nora swallowed. "Actually, your mother dropped off a few groceries for me last week when I couldn't get to the store."

And that would be when she'd been hugging the toilet—her own that time. She was doing way too much of that lately.

"I meant really care for you," he corrected. "I know you're independent, but even you need to rest sometimes."

Nora wanted to sink back into the bed, his bed, but she didn't want to leave the warmth of his firm hand on her shoulder. He was right, though. She was independent. She'd always had to be between her mother and Todd, who'd been deployed most of their brief marriage.

"I don't mind fending for myself, Eli. I've honestly never known any other way."

His hand slid down her arm, leaving gooseflesh in its path even though thick fleece separated them. "That's a sad statement. You will rest here for at least an hour, no arguments. I'll put the casserole in the oven."

"But you are a terrible cook," she insisted. "I remember that Valentine's meal you tried to cook for me that even the stray dogs turned away."

Eli's eyes widened a moment before he chuckled. "That was pretty bad, but you've already thrown the ingredients together. Surely I can pop it in the oven without causing too much damage. I do have a PhD, for pity's sake."

She couldn't help but smile at his accomplishments. "I'm really proud of what you've done, Eli. You had a dream and went after it."

His eyes held hers, the hand he'd slid down her arm rested atop her own. "But at what price?" he whispered.

Her heart clenched. Was he referring to her, to them? Did he regret leaving all those years ago? This was the first inclination he'd ever shown that perhaps he wasn't 100 percent confident in his decisions.

Nora took in his thin lips, his tense shoulders and eyes filled with anguish. Obviously he had his own demons to live with and she didn't feel it her place to say anything.

"I'm sorry I hurt you," he murmured, looking down to their hands. "All those years ago. I never apologized."

Okay, that was a time she did not want to revisit because from the moment he'd left, she'd been seeking happiness, only able to grasp on to meager scraps of it. But she couldn't fully blame him. She was in charge of her own life and had made it what it was—

falling into a marriage with a man who should've remained her friend and nothing more.

"Life happens, Eli." She laced her fingers with his, wanting another layer of connection. "We had different goals in life. Doesn't mean we didn't care for each other. Besides, we were young. We might have made a mistake staying together. You would've probably resented being stuck here and wondered what life outside Stonerock would've been like."

He squeezed her hand back. "I've never known a woman like you, Nora."

She laughed, easing the intensity of the moment. "I'll take that as a compliment."

A wide smile spread across his handsome, stubbled face. "Definitely a compliment."

Silence surrounded them and for the first time it wasn't strained or awkward.

"I'm really glad you're back, Eli."

"I'm not staying."

He was so quick to answer, but she knew he had a life, the one he'd worked so hard for, waiting on him. Good for him for making his life everything he'd ever wanted.

"You're here now," she told him. "That's all that matters."

She didn't want any tension while he was here. First of all, she loved his family too much to have that weighing heavily on them, and second, she couldn't afford the emotional battle.

Even though they were different people than they once were, they could still be friends.

Couldn't they?

Chapter Four

He'd faced the wrath of his father when he'd sneaked out of the house at age fifteen, he'd served alongside men who'd died in front of him and he'd managed to move on after a broken heart.

But nothing scared the hell out of Dr. Eli St. John more than that waiting room full of patients. Patients who remembered the teen he used to be and had no real clue as to the man he'd truly become.

Oh, he wasn't worried about contracting some virus or cold. No, he was terrified the do-gooders of the town would peer down their nose at him and judge him for his past sins.

Eli glanced at his watch and sighed. His father's nurse, Sarah, would start filling the rooms any minute and Eli would just have to suck it up and get this first day out of the way.

At least Sarah was young, new and professional. When he'd walked through the office earlier to speak to Lulu, she'd been filing her nails and the phone had been ringing. It had rung four times before she slammed down her file and answered.

For some reason the townsfolk liked Lulu—with her odd, sometimes rude behavior—and expected her to be sitting behind that desk when they came in. She never changed...ever. And she still sported a low-cut top with her goods on display.

Perhaps that's why she'd always been so well received.

Regardless, Eli's father swore she was the most organized person he'd ever worked with and he'd hired her straight out of high school. Lulu was just shy of forty, a few years older than Eli, so she wasn't going anywhere.

Dr. St. John—the original—was home resting and recovering and depending on Eli to keep the practice afloat. Eli had no intention of letting the man down, no matter what he thought of how his dad ran the office.

Eli moved from his father's small office and went down the narrow hallway, eyeing the closed exam room door. Pulling the chart from the tray, he glanced at the name first...then did a double take.

Perfect. Simply perfect.

Maddie Mays. Or, as he and his brothers called her, "Mad" Maddie. The woman had to be a day older than God himself and she put the fear in every kid who had the unfortunate idea of cutting through her property to the park. More than once Mad Maddie had wielded a rolling pin in one hand and ball bat in the other. There was no doubt the woman would've used both weapons if anyone stepped on her precious prize-winning flowers. Those women in the Flower Garden Club were vicious and Mad Maddie was their president. Don't mess with a woman's rhododendrons.

Too bad she couldn't catch them. Maddie was as wide as she was tall and had certainly been no match for three healthy teen boys.

Eli pushed open the door and for a half second he was shocked. It seemed as though a good one hundred pounds had melted off her. And her wardrobe looked straight out of a sixteen-year-old's closet.

Sitting on the edge of the exam table, Maddie wore hot-pink leggings and a black, fitted, off-the-shoulder sweater. Furry leopard-print boots completed her interesting look. Her cane—which looked as though it had been dipped into a vat of rhinestones—rested against the table.

"Mrs. Mays," he greeted, closing the door for privacy.

When her eyes landed on him, he didn't shudder beneath the gaze that seemed to study and assess him. "Eli. You're quite a bit taller and thicker than last I saw you."

"Yes, ma'am."

Last time she'd seen him he'd been hightailing it past her property after she'd threatened to go get her gun if he touched her pansies again. In his defense, he'd needed a bouquet of flowers for Nora and he'd thought it was dark enough to conceal him. He'd been wrong.

"I'm quite a bit older now," he added, setting her chart on the counter so he could wash his hands in the small sink.

One perfectly penciled-in brow arched. "I hope you've settled down. Are you married?"

"No, ma'am."

Maddie let out a harrumph. "Well, you're not too settled, then."

After drying his hands, he opened the file, more than ready to get down to the reason for her visit. "Mrs. Mays, I'm not showing any symptoms on your chart. I see where Sarah took your vitals, but nothing else."

Eli closed the chart, setting it on the exam table beside her and pulling his stethoscope from around his neck. "Let me just listen to your heart and lungs while you tell me the reason you're here."

"Oh, I'm healthy as a horse, Eli." Maddie smiled when he froze. "Thanks to my vitamins and green tea, I'm healthier now than I was thirty years ago. Of course my workouts help. I had a pole installed in my living room about five years ago after I started reading about all these pole dancers and the strenuous workouts they go through and—"

Eli held up a hand. Besides the fact the dead last thing he wanted to hear about was Maddie and her… pole…he had a more pressing issue.

"Why are you here if you aren't sick?" he asked. "Do you need a refill on any medication?"

"No. Since I started eating healthier a few years ago I was able to get off all my medication. All that processed food will kill you."

Eli took a deep breath, settled his stethoscope back around his shoulders and crossed his arms over his chest.

"Then what can I do for you, Mrs. Mays?"

"I just wanted to have a look-see since you're back in town."

He should've expected this. "Mrs. Mays, I have other patients I need to see. If you're not here for a valid reason, I'll need to get going."

She reached into her oversize purse and pulled out a foil-wrapped package. "I made you a loaf of pumpkin mint bread."

Pumpkin mint?

Eli took the gift, not sure if this was the norm for Maddie. "Thanks," he said as she slid off the exam table.

Maddie clutched her cane and narrowed her eyes. "I'll be keeping my eye on you, Eli. I'm not too comfortable with a St. John boy being my doctor, but I trust your father and he'd never let you into his practice if he didn't think you could do the job."

"I can do the job," he assured her, now wondering if the odd-flavored bread was poisoned.

"Heard you got on at some big hospital in Atlanta." He didn't know how she knew. And that was the crazy thing with small towns. People knew all about your business—occasionally before you did.

"Yes, ma'am."

And if all went well, when he returned it would be to a substantial promotion.

"Well, that's something," she proclaimed as she made her way to the door. "I've been impressed with your brothers, even if they still have that I-don't-give-a-damn attitude."

Eli laughed. "That's something we were born with. But I'd say Drake and Cam have done well for themselves."

Maddie put her hand on the door and turned to smile at him. "You're all still single. You're not doing too well if a woman can't keep hold of you wild boys."

Her laughter followed her down the hall and Eli stood there staring at the empty doorway. What the hell just happened? His first patient wasn't really a patient and in the span of five minutes he'd been given a backhanded compliment, a scary homemade present, a warning and then he was educated on geriatric pole dancing.

Maybe being back in Stonerock wasn't so bad, after all. It certainly wasn't boring and for the past several minutes Nora had stayed out of his mind.

Heading toward home, Nora couldn't help but replay her doctor's appointment. Her BP had been elevated and she was still having some cramping. Thankfully the ultrasound looked good; the baby weighed what she should and her heartbeat was right on track.

A little girl. Nora smiled. Despite the chaos in her life, today she'd been told she would be having a baby girl. For some reason knowing the sex made everything seem so...real. As if the past five months of sickness, fluctuating weight and epic crying sprees hadn't been real enough.

Now Nora would start thinking of names, decorating a nursery, buying cutesy little clothes. Granted, she had to sell her house and find a new one before she could decorate and before the baby came.

No, she needed to go ahead and prepare for the baby. Who knew if or when her house would sell?

Nora sighed. Just the thought of packing up everything and trying to move with a newborn sounded exhausting. But somehow she would trudge on; she had no other option.

If all of that wasn't enough to send her rushing to her freezer for Rocky Road, she also needed to find a replacement vet to fill in for her while she was off.

Was it any wonder her BP had been high? Stress, anyone?

She'd indulged by going to the store and purchasing a ton of fruit...and whipped cream. A girl had to have some guilty pleasure and she really should cut back on the ice cream. But she did pick up another gallon. For emergencies.

Nora pulled into her driveway, resisting the urge to glance over to the St. John residence, all lit up with Christmas lights, wreaths hanging from each window. Their house had always been the picture of perfection. Some families presented only a facade of happiness and togetherness, but Nora knew from experience that even when those doors were closed, that family bond was rock solid.

That's the family life she wanted to provide for her child. Maybe being a single mother wasn't the way she'd envisioned life, but there was no reason she and her baby girl couldn't have their own piece of family perfection.

Smiling, Nora realized she was still staring at the St. John house, daydreaming of the future. She didn't see Eli's truck in the drive, but he may have pulled around back into the garage. If Eli wasn't around, he'd be there shortly if he kept his father's usual office hours and left at six.

And speaking of the St. Johns, she still needed to pick up Christmas presents for her favorite family. With her lack of energy and motivation lately, more than likely she'd be ordering those gifts online.

Darkness had settled in for the night. Nora hated that about winter. It got dark so early, but at least the twinkling Christmas lights from the neighborhood lit up the street.

Of course, she hadn't gotten around to putting up lights yet, but she had hung a pretty evergreen wreath with a bright red-and-white bow on her door and draped some garland over the railing that stretched across her porch. That would have to do for now.

The light snow they'd received the other day had all but melted, but the weatherman was calling for possibly an inch over the next couple days. Just enough to coat the ground and be pretty.

Because she was too tired to try to make multiple trips, Nora juggled her groceries toward the steps to her house.

"Seriously, Nora. Give me those."

She turned to see Eli crossing her driveway. "Get your keys out and I'll carry these in."

"I've got them, Eli," she argued. "I've been bringing in my own food for a while now."

He jerked on the bags, giving her no choice but to relinquish her hold. Stubborn man. Did he honestly think she'd not been able to take care of herself?

"Well, I'm here and I'm cold so open the door."

Nora resisted the urge to roll her eyes; that would be childish. But she did stomp up the steps to her door. Not the most mature behavior, but she couldn't help it. This gorgeous man seemed to be everywhere lately…including her dreams.

What was he doing invading her subconscious? Nostalgia could only go so far. He wasn't the man she'd loved years ago and she certainly wasn't the same woman.

Good grief. As if she even had anything appealing to offer a man! A widowed pregnant lady with a meager income… Seriously, who wouldn't want to get with that?

She unlocked the door and let Eli pass in ahead of her. After she flipped on the lights in the living room and kitchen, she shrugged out of her coat.

"Just throw the bags on the island," she called over

her shoulder as she went into the living room to plug in her Christmas tree. "I'll put everything away."

"I can help put stuff away," he offered.

When she plugged in the tree, she spotted Kerfluffle lying on the red-and-white quilted tree skirt, napping. Her favorite spot this time of year.

She returned to the kitchen and hung her coat on the peg by the back door. She'd just started to hang her purse over the other peg when it slipped from her grasp and fell to the tile, spilling its contents.

She leveled her gaze across the room to Eli. "Really, I'll get it all. But thanks for carrying those groceries in."

Ignoring her subtle dismissal, Eli circled the island and squatted down to help her pick up her purse explosion.

"Eli, I can—"

She froze as he picked up the row of pictures she'd had in her purse from today's ultrasound. The way he stared at each image, the way he slowly straightened his body to come to his full height and the way his eyes finally came to meet hers, Nora knew he wasn't leaving anytime soon.

Chapter Five

Eli couldn't breathe, couldn't speak.

A baby? How the hell did he not know this? He'd been home for five days now and nothing had ever been mentioned. Of course, his father had had heart surgery and his mother was busy with his care, but seriously, he was a doctor—how did he not recognize the fact this woman was pregnant? And far enough along that she knew the sex.

The sickness at his parents', her always hiding beneath her coat, her pale, tired face…all the signs were there.

His eyes traveled from the pictures to her eyes to her belly. With the boxy scrubs she wore at the clinic and her height, she was able to hide her bump.

"Whatever you want to say, just say it," she told

him, taking the pictures from his hands and thrusting her chin up as if she dared him to say anything at all.

He raked a hand over his stubbled jawline. "Honestly, I don't know what to say. Congratulations? How did I not know this? Is the baby…"

Her eyes narrowed. "Thank you. Because you don't know everything about my life, and yes, the baby is Todd's. Whose did you think it would be?"

He hadn't meant to say that, but damn, she'd completely caught him off guard and, with his background, that rarely happened.

"I'm sorry." He studied her another minute, folding his arms across his wide chest and leaning back against the center island. "This is why you were so sick the other day at Mom and Dad's?"

Nora nodded.

Anger bubbled within him. She'd been pushing herself, bending over backward to do it all and… what? To prove she could? To prove she didn't need anybody and she could don the superwoman cape?

"What the hell were you thinking pushing yourself like that?" he demanded, unable to keep his rage fueled by fear locked inside.

"I was thinking I'd help out the two people who've always been like parents to me," she yelled back. "I'm pregnant, Eli, I'm not an invalid. I was getting along fine before you came and I'll continue to do so once you're gone. Just because we had a past doesn't mean you can come in here and start taking charge."

Eli had no idea what to say to that because his anger would only make the situation worse. More than ever, he wanted to protect her, keep her safe, but this wasn't his wife, nor was this his baby.

"Did Todd know about the pregnancy?" he asked.

Nora closed her eyes, shaking her head. "No. He was killed before I found out. I took a home test the day of the funeral."

Eli muttered a curse at the terrible, cruel timing. The pain in her voice sliced through Eli's heart. No wonder she'd been going full speed ahead; she was trying to push beyond the hurt, trying to stay busy so she didn't have to think about the pain. He'd seen this tactic numerous times when he'd been overseas. "I'm sorry I yelled at you."

When her eyes met his again and a soft smile curved her unpainted lips, Eli's breath caught. She was stunning. Not because of the whole girl-next-door appeal she'd always had, but for her strength in all she'd endured through life. The woman before him was so different from the girl he'd left behind. This woman was a warrior.

No matter what fate threw her way, she always smiled as she marched right over any obstacles that would cause most people to give up.

"It's okay," she assured him. "I'm excited about the baby and I know you were shocked. I was pretty shocked, too, when I found out."

That was an understatement, he knew. The timing couldn't have been any worse for her. But at least she didn't know everything about her husband. The secret Eli carried would have to remain hidden because there was no way he'd kill that light in Nora's baby blues. She wanted this little girl, wanted a family, and that's what she'd have. Eli would make sure she kept pleasant memories of Todd with her and passed those down to their baby.

"Did you go to the doctor's appointment alone?" he asked.

Her brows drew together. "Well, yeah. Who else would go with me?"

That right there was the problem. She'd nearly always done things alone.

"I'll go next time."

Great, Eli, just charge right in and take over. Pity and attraction were a bad combination because he wanted to help her from all angles. And he absolutely hated that he felt guilty for Todd's sins.

"I don't need anyone to go with me, Eli," she assured him with another soft smile. "I can handle this on my own."

Not backing down, he moved closer, close enough she had to tip her head slightly to look up at him. He could stare into those mesmerizing eyes forever… If only he'd chosen to stay, where would they be now?

"We're friends, Nora. Let me be there for you while I'm here. With Todd not having any family here, you need someone."

Her eyes widened as she licked her lips. Desire that had nothing to do with the old feelings he had for her twisted in Eli's stomach. Those were gone, those were a lifetime ago.

This thread of attraction was for the woman she

was now, the stubborn, sexy, vibrant woman who kept insisting she didn't need anybody.

"I have friends, Eli." She offered an innocent, sweet smile that didn't quite reach her eyes. "You're here to take care of your father and work. There's no sense in you adding anything else to the mix."

Unable to help himself, Eli reached out, slid a hand across her silky cheek and stroked his thumb across her lower lip.

"Maybe I want to add you to the mix," he murmured as he stepped closer. "Maybe I want to help because you've always had crap thrown at you in life. And maybe I have emotions that won't be ignored."

Nora took a step back, causing his hand to fall away. Her eyes narrowed again and that vulnerability he'd seen only moments ago was replaced by anger.

"I don't want you here out of pity, Eli. I don't need help because you feel sorry for me."

Damn, he was going about this all wrong. Could he be more of a jerk? Friends. That's all they could and would be. The end.

"Nora, please. I'm not offering because I think you're incompetent. I know you're strong and resilient—you wouldn't have gotten this far without that spine of steel you have. Why can't you get that chip off your shoulder and admit you need someone?"

"Because I don't," she said, crossing her arms over her chest. "Your parents are supportive. I realize your dad had major surgery and he'll be recovering for a while, but the moral support they provide is invaluable."

He studied her face, her tilted, defiant chin and her hard stare. "I'm not sure why I'm banging my head against the wall trying to get through that thick head of yours."

Glancing down to the pictures in her hand, his stomach twisted in knots. She was pregnant and he was arguing with her. She'd lost her husband a few months ago, was trying to cope as best as she could and he was making things more difficult.

Eli shook his head and met her gaze once more. "Listen, I'm going to be in town a few months. I may even still be here when your baby is born, depending on Dad's recovery. I want to be your friend. I don't want things to be difficult between us."

"They're not," she countered, her chin starting to quiver. "I just…"

On a sigh she turned her back to him. When she took a deep, shuddering breath, Eli stepped forward. Vulnerable women always got him, but Nora had always been so strong. Granted, he hadn't seen her for years, but she'd been so determined to put him in his place and convince him she needed nobody.

When he wrapped his hands around her, cupping her slender shoulders, she fell back against his chest. The top of her head came to rest just below his chin and he couldn't stop himself from inhaling her sweet, floral scent.

"It's so hard to see you, Eli," she whispered. "When I see you, I think of Todd. To know he'll never see his child is…hard."

Eli's heart sank. Of course she was still torn up

over her deceased husband. Why wouldn't she be? She had no idea the man he truly was and Eli sure as hell wouldn't be the one to tell her because if Nora thought her husband died a hero, a good husband, then he'd let her live that dream.

And Todd's secret would die with Eli.

"I'm sorry," he told her, turning her to face him. "I'm sorry if seeing me is painful. I can keep my distance. I guess I wasn't thinking."

"No, we were friends and you'll be staying here for months. I'm coming to terms with Todd being gone. I just hate that our baby will never know her father." She tilted her chin and blinked back unshed tears. "Besides, you're right next door and I'm always visiting Bev and Mac."

After wiping her hands on her scrub top, she smiled. "Sorry. I'm a little more emotional lately with the pregnancy."

Eli reached out, sliding his thumb over her silky cheek. "Never apologize to me for being who you are, Nora. If you need to cry, there's nothing to be ashamed of. Don't try to hold back."

"I can't cry," she told him, shaking her head. "I'm so afraid if I start, I won't be able to stop."

When she reached up to lay her hand on his chest, her familiar warmth slid all the way through his body. At one time those delicate hands had been all over him. Now, though, he couldn't let current desires override common sense. He wasn't the horny teen with very little self-control he'd once been.

Besides, he was leaving as soon as he got the green light from his father. And possibly the biggest promotion of his career was waiting for him back in Atlanta.

"Why don't you stay for dinner?" she offered.

He took in the exhaustion in her dark eyes, the fatigue that had her shoulders just a little slumped.

"Only if you go change and have a seat in the living room." He offered her a smile. "I'll look through here and make us dinner."

She shook her head. "Eli, no. I'm not asking you to make my dinner. I'm perfectly—"

"Capable," he cut her off. "I know. But I need to eat and you need to change. You can put the groceries away while I'm cooking and we'll get everything done faster."

Her mouth twisted as she considered his proposal. He wouldn't beg, but he wouldn't leave until he knew she was taken care of for the evening whether she liked it or not.

"I guess that would be all right," she conceded. "Thanks."

Eli shouldn't feel so thrilled about making dinner, but he was. Once he'd gotten into her house he didn't want to leave, and now that he knew she was pregnant, he sure as hell would be keeping a closer watch on her.

Maybe Todd wasn't the husband he should've been, but he had been Eli's best friend and Eli felt it his duty to watch over Nora and her unborn child. There was no way he could just walk away from Nora now…

especially considering those newfound lustful feelings weighing heavy in his gut.

"I'll go change real quick before I put this stuff away," she told him. "Be right back."

As she turned to walk from the kitchen, Eli clenched his fists, trying to gain control over his emotions. Anything beyond friendship with Nora was off the table. She'd nearly cried in his arms for her late husband, the father of her baby, but he got the sense she wouldn't fully allow herself that luxury.

Eli had no place in her personal life; he'd lost that right when he'd given her up to join the service and get his doctorate with a naive innocence that he could somehow make the world a better place. He'd wanted to follow in his father's footsteps and join the army, no matter what he had to sacrifice at home to follow his dream.

When being a soldier hadn't satisfied him enough, he'd decided to continue his father's career path and get his medical degree in the military. If he couldn't save the world, he'd save patients, one trauma at a time.

Which was why he needed to focus on his main goal of getting back to Atlanta, back to the possibility of being the head doctor in the trauma unit. Nothing else could distract him. But that wouldn't stop Eli from keeping watch over Nora while he was here.

Eli pulled open the fridge to see what all he had to work with. By the time he'd gotten his hormones in check and his head on straight, Nora came waltzing back into the kitchen wearing snug black leggings and an off-the-shoulder sweatshirt. That creamy, slender shoulder shouldn't be so provocative, but it was and all thoughts of anything else went out the window as he prepared dinner with the only woman he'd ever wanted.

Chapter Six

"I have to admit, that was amazing."

Nora started up her dishwasher and turned to Eli, who was putting the lid on the leftovers. All of this seemed a little too domestic, but she had to remain in control of her feelings, especially since she'd nearly broken down in his arms earlier.

She wasn't lying about it being hard to see him because she thought of Todd, but that wasn't the real reason. How could she not acknowledge the underlying emotions? Not old, young-love emotions, but new, budding ones that stemmed from something fresh. The man before her was not the same boy who left with stars in his eyes and a cocky attitude. This man was harsher, more intriguing, yet proud and determined.

Even if she'd just met him and they had no history, Nora would be attracted to Dr. Eli St. John.

"Hey, you okay?" Eli asked, coming to stand in front of her.

"I'm fine." She offered him a smile and leaned back against the kitchen counter. "Thanks so much for dinner. It's not often someone cooks for me, unless it's your mother."

"Then I'll have to be sure to do it again while I'm here," he told her, offering a grin of his own.

That heart-clenching smile shot straight to her core. He'd always had a smug yet handsome smile as a teen, but now as a full-grown man with creases around his mouth and soft wrinkles at the edge of his eyes, he was even more devastatingly handsome and flat-out sexy.

But could she even trust what she was feeling when her emotions were already heightened from the pregnancy and the whirlwind of Todd's death? Granted, her husband had filed for divorce before he was killed, and she'd had no idea until the papers arrived in the mail a day after she'd found out she'd lost him for good, but she had been in a committed relationship even if the marriage hadn't been the best. Nora had wanted to make it work because she wasn't a quitter and she'd dreamed of having a family of her own her entire life.

She and Todd had been more friends than anything and looking back she realized they were both hoping for something the other simply couldn't give.

She'd even tried to put a spark into their marriage

by seducing him that last night he'd been home on leave…hence the pregnancy.

If she was honest with herself, she'd never felt this strong of a bond, an attraction, to Todd the way she did with Eli. But now…well, they had so many more barriers between them. She had a baby to think of first and foremost.

"I have to say, having a handsome man cook for me isn't something I'll turn down," she told him, settling her hands beside her on the edge of the counter.

"Then we'll have to make it a weekly thing." Eli cocked his head and studied her. "What night works best for you?"

Nora shrugged, glad they were finally on a comfortable topic. "I leave the clinic later on Thursday so having dinner that night would be great since that's my long day."

"Thursday, it is."

"What about your schedule?" she asked. "Are you free that evening."

"I'll make it work."

His quick response and lack of worry melted her heart. He didn't have to reach out to her, didn't have to adjust his temporary life here to make hers easier. Yet he was and he truly didn't mind.

"You don't know what this means to me, Eli."

Those dark eyes roamed over her face as he stepped forward. Nora tipped her head up to hold his gaze and found herself mesmerized by the scar. Not the physical aspect of it, but the story behind it— the story she didn't know. Just that alone symbolized how so much had changed between them—so much she knew nothing about.

"I want you to be able to relax and concentrate on this pregnancy and yourself," he stated in that doctor tone she'd become familiar with. "And I don't say that out of pity. I say that because you're always helping everyone else and you deserve to be pampered a bit yourself."

Pampered? She didn't even know what that meant anymore.

"I should probably get back home and see what Mom and Dad need from me."

Nora nodded, a bit disappointed that he was leaving, yet knowing it was for the best. The more time she spent with him, the more she'd want to spend with him. She walked him to her front door. Bright white light from the Christmas tree filled the room, illuminating Kerfluffle, who was still asleep on the tree skirt. The crisp glow from the tree spilled into the darkened foyer. Nora reached for the knob just as Eli reached around her to do the same.

From behind, his body molded to hers. Nora sucked in a breath as shivers raced through her body. He didn't bother to move, to step back or remove his hand that covered hers. She didn't want to relish this simple moment, but she couldn't stop herself from taking in the exact feel of his body pressed so intimately to hers.

Eli had leaned in farther, his warm breath tickling her neck. There was no way to avoid the temptation spreading to every tingling part of her body.

"You still smell like flowers, Nora," he whispered. "It's just one of the things I remember about you."

Nora closed her eyes as his low tone washed over her, through her.

"When I first deployed, I'd lie awake in my bunk and think back to your sweet smell," he went on in that sultry tone. "I used any distraction I could to get through it. And nearly every mental tactic involved you."

Nora couldn't do this, couldn't listen to his memories wrapped and delivered in that smooth, soft voice. No matter how her body responded to his touch, she couldn't let him affect her on such an intimate level anymore.

"Eli, don't," she whispered.

His free hand came up to cup her shoulder. The strength from just that simple touch radiated through her and she wished she could draw more from him, wished she could be this open about her own emotions, her fears.

But she had to be cautious because where her emotions led, her heart tended to follow, and right now her heart had taken enough of a beating. As much as Eli intrigued her on so many levels—namely the lustful one—she couldn't get wrapped up in a man who had every intention of leaving.

Eli slid his hand down her arm, removed his other hand from hers off the doorknob. Nora turned, but he hadn't stepped back and she had to tip her head to look at him. She'd always been tall for a girl, but Eli was all man—big, powerful, muscular. Even with his dominating presence, she always felt protected, safe, cherished.

"I didn't mean to make you uncomfortable," he told her. "I look at you and see the girl I loved. I smell flowers and remember how you always had some floral lotion on."

The soft lights from the living room projected a glow around his entire body, framing his broad shoulders, his tipped head. She often forgot that Eli had served and seen just as much as Todd had. So many times Todd would have nightmares when he'd be home on leave and she'd have to console him, comfort him.

Who did that for Eli? He had to have had bad moments, times that haunted him. Had there ever been a special someone in his life to get him through rough times?

"I'm not uncomfortable." A small lie. "We're both just so vulnerable right now and so different from the kids we used to be. Between you with your dad and the practice, and me with the baby, there's just so much stress."

"What can I do to make things easier for you?" he asked, searching her eyes. "I may only be here a few months, but we're friends, Nora. I want to help. Do you need the nursery painted? Crib put together?"

A vice-grip tightened around her heart. She didn't want to feel anything toward Eli beyond friendship. But after he'd opened up and shared a small portion of his time overseas and the fact he was obviously waging some internal battle with himself, Nora found herself getting more and more entangled in his world.

"I'll be sure to let you know when I need any of that stuff done," she promised, finding that she probably would take him up on such a generous offer.

Eli reached up, pushed a stray strand of hair behind her ear. "This little girl is one lucky baby to have you for her mom."

Nora smiled. "I'm the lucky one. A little nervous, but lucky."

"Nothing to be nervous about," he assured her, his hand still lingering by her neck. "You'll be an amazing mother."

"Who do I have to compare myself to? My mother…" Nora sighed, not wanting to get into that particular part of her life.

Eli's hands cupped her face, forcing her to look him straight in the eye. "It's because of your mother that you'll be so wonderful. You know how it feels to be abandoned, to crave love and stability."

Nora couldn't help but get lost in his words, those dark eyes and his conviction. He was the only man who ever really got her, and even though a gap of years stood between them, he still understood her.

"Plus you've always looked up to my parents," he added with a slight grin. "You've got great role models. Me and my brothers turned out all right."

"After a few mishaps." She laughed.

Eli shrugged. "Just a few."

His thumbs stroked her cheeks and Nora brought her hands up to wrap around his wrists. She couldn't find the strength to push him away. If she were honest with herself, she loved having him there, but she also had to face reality, and that cold hard truth was he wouldn't always be there.

For now, Nora would take comfort from him for as long as he was willing to give it. Maybe that made her weak, but with all that was going on, she just didn't have the strength to fight his pull.

"I'm just next door if you need anything," he murmured.

Nora nodded, unable to speak with his lips so close. Why did he have to still appeal to her? Why was she still drawn to the town-bad-boy-turned-soldier-turned-doctor…turned devastatingly sexy, intriguing, unattainable man?

"I'll check on you after work, Nora."

She knew it was coming; she had ample time to stop him…but she didn't want to.

Eli's lips touched hers, softly, tenderly. Before she could fully appreciate the familiar touch, he backed away.

"See you tomorrow."

When he reached around her to open the door, Nora stepped out of the way. Once she was alone, she couldn't stop her fingers from drifting to her lips, trying to capture that feeling of his kiss.

Eli was going to be in town for a few months and she'd already tasted his lips. What would getting more attached to him do to her mental state?

Kissing Eli may be one of the sweetest things ever, but nothing good would come from it. Nothing.

Nora walked back through her kitchen to turn the lights off before heading upstairs to bed.

After changing into her nightgown and collapsing into bed, Nora remembered she hadn't talked to Eli about a surprise anniversary party for his parents in the new year. And that was the main reason she'd wanted him to stay for dinner.

Proof that the man had her mind solely focused on him and not reality or priorities.

Yeah, she was in big trouble.

Treating patients' ailments was damn hard when all Eli could think of was the kiss he'd shared with Nora. Granted, it was little more than a peck, but he'd touched her, tasted her and his body had responded.

So far he'd seen two cases of strep, one case of a basic cold and filled a few prescriptions. Nothing exciting, everything very mundane in Stonerock. Not that he wished anyone to get hurt, but as a doctor and ex-military he thrived on the adrenaline rush of the traumas. He had a natural calling to heal people.

Perhaps that's just another reason Nora pulled at him in her current state. He'd sensed a thread of vulnerability in her, but once he'd learned of the pregnancy he realized just how vulnerable she truly was.

Eli closed the door to his father's small office in the back of the clinic. It was lunchtime and he needed a few minutes to himself.

Todd had been a great friend, even better soldier, but he'd been a terrible, selfish husband. And a good part of Eli was angry Todd had left Nora behind, alone and pregnant.

Eli knew full well Todd had sacrificed himself for his country, but the man would've never done so much for his own family. If he were alive today, Eli seriously doubted Todd would stick around to play husband and daddy.

Eli hated the bitterness that rolled through him and he really needed to get a grasp on this situation. Right now, all that was important was Nora—her comfort, the baby—and taking care of his father.

Unfortunately his mind kept returning to the last night he and Todd had spent together. Absently Eli reached up to trace the scar, a visible reminder of how ugly jealousy could be.

When his cell rang, Eli pulled it from his lab coat pocket and smiled. A reprieve, thank God.

"Hey, Cam," he answered.

"Bad time?" his brother asked.

"Not at all. What's up?"

"You talked to Nora today?"

At his brother's serious tone, Eli sat up straighter in his chair. "No, why?"

"Her clinic was broken into. We just got everything all straightened out and cleaned up."

Jerking to his feet, Eli was grabbing his keys from the desk drawer. "Was she hurt?"

Fear raced through him at the thought of her or her baby being injured. This was certainly not the type of adrenaline he'd been hoping for. *Be careful what you wish for.*

"She's fine. Angry, but fine," Cameron assured him. "She came to work and found the back door open."

Eli sighed, closing his eyes. "Tell me she didn't go in and check it out before calling you."

On the other end, Cameron laughed. "She may be stubborn, but she's not stupid. She called me and I went in to make sure the perp was gone. Then she went through and we made a list of all that had been taken."

Eli took off his lab coat and hung it on the peg by the exit. "What on earth would someone want from a vet's office?"

"Syringes. Nora's office was easier to break into than a drugstore and the druggies are desperate. They'll take things any way they can get them."

No longer relegated to big cities, the drug problem had unfortunately trickled into small-town America, causing damage to so many lives, ruining too many families.

"I'm on my way," Eli told his brother. "Tell her to sit tight."

"No need for you to leave work, Eli. She's fine. I swear."

Yeah, well, her world had been shaken—again— and he intended to go support her. Pain didn't always come in the physical form.

"I'm on my way," he repeated. "It's not up for debate."

Eli hung up his phone before his brother could argue further. There was no reason for him not to go to her. Well, his patients were several reasons, actually. He'd have to reschedule if he couldn't get back before his lunch break was over.

When he moved into the front office, Lulu was finishing a salad at her desk. Eli had to blink several times to keep his attention away from the massive cleavage she had on display, outlined by rhinestones riding the edge of her V-neck.

"I'll be out for the afternoon," he told her, quickly deciding he needed to stay with Nora. "If there's an emergency, call my cell and I can come back. I need you to reschedule today's patients. Squeeze them in tomorrow, even if I have to work later."

Her brows drew together. "Oh, honey. Everything okay? Your dad…"

"He's fine. Nora's clinic was broken into."

"I heard that when I went out to get my salad," she told him, grabbing her nail file from the desk. "Crazy people always wanting to steal instead of working for an honest living. Go ahead. This afternoon was very light, anyway."

She started sharpening her bloodred nails into dangerous-looking daggers. When the phone started ringing, she blew on one finger and stared, filing another.

"You going to get that?" he asked.

Without looking up, she nodded. "I don't tell you how to do your job. Now go on and see to your veterinarian friend."

Sighing, Eli wasn't getting into the annoyances

that surrounded his father's receptionist. "I'll see you in the morning."

Eli grabbed his coat and keys as he rushed out the back door, the frigid air cutting through him. December was downright freezing, unusually cold for Tennessee, but better than the blizzard-like conditions up north.

In no time he'd gone from one end of the tiny town to the other and pulled behind Nora's clinic. His brother's cruiser was parked right outside the back door. Eli killed the engine on his truck and headed toward the back entrance. Before he could step inside, the metal door swung open.

"I knew you'd show up as soon as you heard." Nora stood in the doorway with her arms crossed over her chest. "I'm surprised it took you this long to hear about the break-in."

"Cam called me," he told her as he stepped inside, forcing her to step back. "You okay?"

She nodded, biting her lip. "I'm just angry. I work too hard and I really don't have time for this. The money I lost today from not working really is what irks me the most. But at least I rescheduled my patients."

Money? She was worried about money? Todd had always talked about all the savings he'd set aside. Did Nora not have those funds or had she already spent them? The VA had surely covered the funeral expenses. What about Todd's pension?

"What do you need me to do?" he asked. "Did they tear up anything?"

"Nothing much. My medicine cabinet was broken into, so I need a new lock. Obviously the perp knew exactly what they wanted. I'm just thankful none of the animals were hurt."

Eli walked through the narrow hallway, glancing into the side rooms. Kennels sat in one oversize room, and only half were full. One dog snoozed as if his world hadn't changed one bit, another puppy was pawing through the cage trying to seek the attention of said snoozing dog and another mini-dog started growling when Eli popped his head in.

"Oh, Harvard, you're fine," Nora said, stepping into the room. "He's harmless."

Eli laughed. "Harvard?"

Nora threw a glance over her shoulder "It's Professor Wilkes's dog."

Professor Wilkes taught at the community college, and rumor had it he'd had the opportunity to teach at a prestigious Ivy League school, but he turned it down because his wife was from this area and he'd wanted to stay with her. He had since been widowed, but remained teaching at the small college in dinky little Stonerock.

Nora quickly fed the dogs and moved to the other side of the room where the cats were starting to meow, obviously eager for some lunch, as well.

"You can go on back to work, Eli. I'm just going to run to the hardware store, grab some new locks and come back and install them."

"I'll do it."

She closed the last cage, her hand resting on the

latch as she quirked a brow at him. "Seriously, I know how to change locks. No sense in both of us missing a day's work."

Eli shoved his hands in his jacket pockets and leaned against the doorway. "I'm sure you do know how, but you can change the cabinet and get that squared away and I can work on the doors. We'll get this done twice as fast. I'm sure you'll need to reorder supplies, which I don't know how to do, so let me help you."

Nora opened her mouth, no doubt to argue, but stopped. Her hand went to her belly as she froze; her eyes widened. Eli was across the room in two strides, his hand coming to rest on hers, his other on her back for support.

"Nora? What's wrong?"

Fear consumed him as she remained silent. Was she in pain? Something wrong with the baby? God, as a doctor, the endless possibilities flooded his mind.

"I've never felt her kick that hard." She laughed. "Just surprised me."

Tension rolled off his shoulders as he exhaled the breath he hadn't realized he'd been holding. "Doesn't she kick at lot at this stage?" he asked. Babies were certainly not his area of expertise, but he did know enough to be concerned when a woman clutched her abdomen and nearly doubled over.

Nora shook her head. "Not really. The doctor said she would start getting more active, but this was so… obvious."

She smiled, looking up to him with a vibrant sparkle in her eyes. "Here," she said, sliding her hand over and placing his on her slightly rounded belly. "Maybe she'll do it again."

Eli waited, wanting to feel this new life, but at the same time wondering if the guilt card would show its face again. This was Todd's position, not Eli's. Todd wasn't here, though, and Nora wanted someone to share in this milestone moment.

As Nora watched his face, waiting for the kick and a reaction from him, he knew he wouldn't want to be anywhere else. He also knew that fate had handed him this opportunity and he would seize it with both hands.

The gentle movement beneath his palm may have been subtle, but it shot straight to his heart. Eli's eyes sought Nora's and her smile widened.

"That's amazing," he whispered. "I mean, I've felt babies kick before, but knowing this is your baby…"

He had no words. Nora's baby, a little girl moving beneath his hands. It was enough to have his own throat clogging with tears.

Damn, he felt as if he were the expectant daddy. How absurd was that?

"Thank you," he told her, sliding his hand away. "I've never been part of something so personal and incredible."

Nora placed both of her hands on her abdomen. "I'm glad you were here. Sharing this pregnancy with friends makes it even more special."

Friends. Yes. He'd do good to keep that solid fact in the forefront of his mind. Nora most definitely had enough on her plate without contending with his advances. And didn't he have enough to keep himself occupied, as well?

"What do you say we hit the hardware store?" he asked.

"Can we grab lunch first? I'm starving."

Eli nodded. "You read my mind."

As he escorted her out, he reiterated to himself that friends were all they were, all they could be. Then why did he want to spend his every waking minute with her and rediscovering the new Nora?

Eli escorted her through the lot and up into his four-wheel-drive truck. As long as he was here, he would stick close to her, allow himself the luxury of being her friend. He might want more, but he would take what he could get.

And in the end, he'd walk away.

Chapter Seven

"In all my years I only closed the clinic early twice."

Eli set his father's plate of grilled chicken and steamed vegetables on a tray in front of the old recliner where Mac had been stationed since being released from the hospital. He'd known his father wouldn't be too pleased with the fact Eli left early, but Nora had come first. For once in his life, he was making her needs his top priority. He doubted many people had ever put her first.

"Once was when Drake broke his arm and had to have surgery," Mac went on. "And the other time was when you and your brothers decided to spray graffiti on the railroad overpass and I had to do damage control with the chief *and* the mayor."

Eli stood back, resting his hands on his hips. "Am I going to get scolded?" he joked with a smile.

Mac looked up, pointing his fork. "Don't get smart with me, young man. I'm simply stating that I only closed for emergencies and when I was needed."

Eli waited, glancing at his mother as she came in and took a seat on the sofa with her own dinner. Just like old times, she tried to stay out of arguments, but Eli knew she'd already formed an opinion.

"I'd say what you did today was exactly what I would've done," his father said before stabbing a piece of chicken. "Nora really has nobody in her life and I'm glad you're here for her."

Raking a hand over his hair, Eli sank into the accent chair across the room. "I came back for *you*, Dad."

His father raised his bushy brows and eyed him across the room. No words were spoken, none needed to be. Mac St. John knew where his son stood.

But his father didn't know how seeing Nora all grown up and sexier than ever had taken a major toll on Eli's nerves. He was having a hard time denying the fact he wanted to spend more time with her and get to know her all over again.

"How is Nora after the break-in?" his mom asked.

Eli eased back against the cushion and nodded. "She's okay. Angry, but she's fine. Was more worried about the animals than her clinic. None of them were injured, thank God. We would've seen a whole new level of mad had something happened to one of her pets or patients."

Bev smiled as she picked up her tea. "Sounds like her. Always looking out for everyone but herself."

"I'm looking out for her," Eli found himself saying before he could think. Damn it.

"Of course you are." Mac nodded his approval. "I knew when you were coming home you'd be spending more time with her than here."

Eli opened his mouth, but shut it as his father held up a hand.

"I'm not saying that bothers me. In fact, I'm glad she has you." He motioned to Bev with his fork. "She's capable of taking care of me. You're needed more with Nora and the clinic."

"Why didn't either of you tell me she was pregnant?" Eli asked, looking between his mother and father.

Mac dug back into dinner while his mother eased her fork down, gently dabbed at her mouth with her napkin as if she were sitting at a grand dining table rather than a TV tray in her living room. Neither parent met his gaze.

"We knew Nora would tell you," Bev informed him. "She was pretty upset when she discovered the pregnancy, not because of the baby itself, but because of the timing."

Eli completely understood and couldn't even fathom what Nora must've felt, and was still feeling, burying her husband and discovering the pregnancy in the same day. The woman was stronger than most men he'd been in the service with.

"She's having a girl," Eli said.

His mother's smile lit up her entire face. "Oh, she'll be such a wonderful mother. I can't wait to buy stuff for that sweet baby."

Eli rolled his eyes, knowing his mother was already mentally shopping. "No need to go overboard, Mom."

"If I want to go overboard with buying precious baby things for Nora and her little girl, then I most certainly will. Besides, that's the closest I'll probably ever come to having a grandchild."

Eli knew his mother meant the statement playfully, but a part of him took it personally. Yes, he and his brothers were not ready to settle down, but at one time Eli thought he'd marry and have children with Nora.

"Nora wouldn't be able to do this without you guys so close," he told his mom. "I know she's independent, but she's still vulnerable."

After his parents finished eating, Eli got his father his medicine and joined his mother in the kitchen as they cleaned up the dishes. "You've been seeing Nora quite a bit," his mother mentioned in that casual yet nosy tone.

Eli shrugged and added the plates to the dishwasher. "She's my friend. I care about her."

"I always figured she'd marry one of my boys. You were definitely the front runner, but when you left, I was certain Drake or Cameron would scoop her up."

Resting his hand on the edge of the countertop, Eli laughed. "Maybe she didn't want to be 'scooped' by either of my brothers."

Bev wiped her hands on an old plaid kitchen towel

and folded it neatly on the counter before turning to face him. "What I meant was, I always considered her one of my own and selfishly I'd hoped she'd be part of our family...officially."

Eli wasn't quite comfortable with this particular topic. At one time he'd assumed Nora would be part of his family, too, but he'd made the choice to leave Stonerock and she'd made the choice to stay.

As teens they'd been in love, as much as teens could be, and had dreams like any other young couple. Then reality and goals flushed to the surface, leaving them no choice but to end their relationship.

That had been one of the hardest moments of his life. The second hardest was when she'd married Todd.

"It's never too late," his mother told him in that soft tone of hers. She offered a smile, causing the wrinkles around her eyes to deepen. "I know you still hold a special place in your heart for her."

Yes, he did. But not nearly the same way or level he had when he'd been eighteen. This was so much more...intense and complicated.

"I'll always care for her."

Bev's head tilted, her eyes softened. "Then why don't you see where this will go while you're home? You never know what could happen in a few months' time. Plus with the holidays it's the perfect opportunity to get closer to her."

Eli raked a hand through his hair and sighed. "Because the end result will be the same, Mom. I'm going back to Atlanta. I hope to get that promotion and I just purchased a new condo. I really like the life I've started."

"You haven't mentioned any friends or girlfriends since you've been home. Just sounds like a lonely new life to me," she muttered, but driving her point home just the same. "But I'm proud of you, of your achievements."

Eli lifted the dishwasher door, closed it and reached out to hug his mother. "Some of us just aren't meant to have long, happy marriages like you and Dad."

Her tiny arms came around his waist. "I know, but I want the best for my boys."

Eli heard the unspoken words: Nora was the best… for him.

Bev eased back, looked up to Eli and smiled. "I'm just glad you're here now. I could've cared for your father on my own, but he was so worried about his clinic."

Eli returned her grin. "I wouldn't be anywhere else, Mom. You can always count on me."

"Such a suck-up."

Eli and his mom both turned to the doorway where Drake stood with his hands in his coat pocket.

Eli hugged his mother tighter. "You're just upset because I'm her favorite."

Drake flipped him the bird.

"Drake Michael," their mother scolded. "Not in my presence. Mind your manners."

Drake crossed the room and kissed his mother on her cheek as Eli let go.

"I'm too old to be punished," he joked. "Besides,

I just had a rough couple of days at work. I blame all bad behavior on sleep deprivation."

"Too many cats in trees?" Eli joked.

Drake laughed. "Funny. How many snotty noses did you treat today?"

Eli crossed his arms over his chest. "Two, actually, and it would've been more but I was called away to Nora's clinic because of a break-in."

"Is Nora okay?" Drake asked, suddenly not joking or smiling.

"She's fine," Eli assured him. "Happened before she arrived and they only took meds from the cabinet."

"Odd," Drake said, shrugging out of his coat and hanging it on the back of a kitchen chair. "Why break in there?"

"Cam says she's an easy target," Eli said. "She has no alarm system. Pharmacies do and Dad's office does. Of course, Dad's office doesn't have anything of major street value, but we have the supplies."

"What did Nora have?" Drake asked.

"Syringes," Eli told him. "Anything to assist in getting high or to sell. They targeted her clinic because of the lack of alarm and no one would think of that."

Drake nodded. "What else does Cam think?"

"Cameron has been working on some undercover case," their mother chimed in, sliding her silvery hair across her forehead and behind her ear. "He's been so busy and secretive. Was he on the scene today?"

Eli nodded. "He left just after I got there. He must

be busy because he hasn't been around here lately and he rarely answers my texts."

Bev hugged her arms over her abdomen. "I worry for him. For all my boys, but whatever he's working on really has him tied off from us. It's never been like that with him before."

Eli threw Drake a glance, but his brother just shrugged. Obviously Drake didn't know what Cam was working on, either. Eli added that to his list of things to do. He would talk to Cam, if nothing else, to give their mother peace of mind.

"I'm sure he's fine, Mom." Eli kissed his mother on the forehead. "There are some things he just can't discuss. We know he's careful. He's the chief of police, for crying out loud. His officers won't let anything happen to him."

Bev smiled, but he knew she wasn't convinced. "You going to be here awhile?" Eli asked Drake.

"Yeah."

Eli grabbed his coat from beneath Drake's on the kitchen chair. "I need to run out and do some things. I'll be back later."

"Tell Nora I said hi." Drake laughed.

Eli threw him the bird as he opened the door.

"Eli Ryan," his mother shouted as he closed the door behind him.

So what if he was going to see Nora? He had some things he wanted to discuss with her and, well, he just wanted to see her.

There, he could admit that he had a problem. And

the problem was the tall, curvy woman who had worked her way back into his life without even trying.

"Do you always make home visits to victims?" Nora joked.

Cameron laughed as he wrapped his arms around her. "Only the pretty ones."

Stepping back and gesturing for him to have a seat, Nora hung his coat by the door. "Eli and I installed new locks today."

"That's good." Cameron crossed his ankle over his knee. "What about an alarm system?"

Nora crossed her arms, shaking her head. "I've thought of that, but the expense is pretty steep. Even if I could do the installation and setup, there's the monthly fee. Besides, I'm sure this isn't going to be a recurring thing."

Cameron nodded. "Most often criminals don't come back to the exact scene, but you're an easy target. With no alarm system, they aren't going to think twice about getting back in."

Nora sighed and sank down onto the sofa beside Cameron. "I'll think about it, but it's just not in the budget right now."

"You know me, Eli, Mom and Dad—"

Nora shook her head. "I'm not asking for money. It will be fine. Besides, I've been talking to a real estate agent about selling this house. If I can downsize, I'll have a little extra to put toward the clinic."

"Why are you selling?" he asked, brows drawn down.

Settling a hand over her belly where the baby was

moving slightly, Nora shrugged. "It's too big for me and the baby. Too much to worry about, try to keep up with. I know Todd was gone a lot, but when he was here he managed to keep it in good shape. I just don't have the time or money for all of that now."

Cameron eased forward on the sofa and turned to fully face her. "Anytime you need anything done here all you have to do is ask. Drake and I will be here in a second."

Nora patted his leg. "You guys have your own lives. I can't call every time the faucet leaks or my grass needs to be cut."

A knock on her front door cut into their conversation and Kerfluffle perked up from her favorite resting spot beneath the Christmas tree.

When Nora skirted around the coffee table and went to look out the sidelight, she smiled. Eli on her porch wrapped in his coat was a sight she'd never tire of seeing.

She opened the door to a cold blast of air and Eli with his wide shoulders filling the entryway. "Come on in," she said, stepping aside. "It's becoming a St. John reunion."

"I saw his unmarked car in your driveway." Eli shrugged out of his coat, hanging it by her door. "Shouldn't you be catching criminals?"

Cameron smiled, flashing that killer grin that ladies loved. "Even the chief has to take a break."

"Do either of you want anything to eat or drink?" Nora asked, suddenly feeling like she should play the hostess.

Eli took her hand, guided her to the vacant chair across from the sofa and eased her down. "We don't want anything and you need to be resting."

Nora rolled her eyes. "I'm not dying, Eli. I'm pregnant. You're a doctor—surely you know all of this already."

Cameron laughed. "You really should take care of yourself. We want a healthy baby in April."

While she hated being told what to do, Nora had to admit that being ordered around and protected by such handsome, sexy men did have its perks. Who was she to argue?

As soon as she was seated, Kerfluffle darted over to Nora's lap and stretched out, obviously ready for some love. Why was the affection always on the cat's terms? Did she own the house?

"Now that you're here, I'll head on out." Cameron came to his feet. "I need to run by the station before I go home."

"You might as well throw a cot in your office and sell your house," Eli commented. "And pop in over at Mom and Dad's because Mom was just saying how she hasn't seen you. She's worried."

Cameron rubbed a hand over his face. His lids drooped and frown lines were becoming more evident. Whatever he was working on was draining the life out of him. Nora wanted him to relax and take some time off, but he was the chief and she highly doubted he'd ever get enough time off to truly benefit him.

"I'll stop in," he told Eli. "Nora, please call me

anytime. If you hear anything about the break-in or if you need something done around here. Don't sell just yet, okay?"

Eli's head whipped around. "Sell?"

Grabbing his own coat by the door, Cameron laughed. "And that's my cue to leave."

Nora crossed her legs, rested one hand on her growing belly while the other stroked her tabby. "Stop staring at me, Eli. The Neanderthal thing is getting old."

Resting his hands on his narrow hips, Eli continued to glare down at her. "Why are you moving? Todd always told me how much you loved this house."

Nora closed her eyes, tipping her head back to rest on the cushion of the chair. "I do. But I can't keep up, and with only one income, it's just too much. The money from the VA went to the funeral. Todd had a meager savings, but apparently he had racked up some debt with a couple credit cards that I knew nothing about so the savings went to that. I'm just bouncing the idea around. It's a hard decision."

Suddenly Eli was beside her, sliding his strong fingers over hers. Nora stared at the image of his dark, scarred hands over her pale, delicate ones. When her eyes came up to meet his, she saw pain.

"I'm sorry, Nora. I know you guys shared some good times here—"

Nora couldn't help the onslaught of tears as she shook her head. "No, we didn't. That's just it. There were no good times, Eli."

Stupid pregnancy hormones. She hadn't meant to

blurt out the ugly truth hiding between these walls. The life she and Todd shared wasn't picture-perfect, and while she'd love to blame him for the disaster that was their marriage, she had to be honest and take half of that blame. They were two loving people who never should've gotten married. Two people who should've remained friends and nothing more.

"Nora." Eli reached up, cupping her face until she fully focused on him. "I'm not sure what went on with you and Todd, but I know he would want you to be happy."

Oh, he had loved her in his own way, but not enough to stay married. Knowing that he wanted out of their marriage hurt her in a way she hadn't expected. But it was his death, so abrupt, so final, that nearly killed her.

This baby was giving her new hope and there was no way she would let her little girl down. Unlike her own free-spirited mother.

"I'll find a way to help you keep your house," he vowed. "Trust me."

"I don't want to talk about this," she whispered. "I'm sorry."

Sighing, Nora closed her eyes, not wanting him to see her own pain…her growing feelings toward him.

"You must think I'm the weakest person." She laughed. "Every time you're around I'm an emotional mess. I swear it's the hormones."

Eli gripped her hands again and smiled. That smile lived in her mind, her heart. That warm smile never failed to make her happier and bring back memories of better times.

"You're one of the strongest people I know," he told her. "Man or woman. You get crap thrown at you and still continue to come out on top."

Yeah, well, she felt like she was at the bottom of that crap pile and slowly crawling her way out.

As she raised her gaze to Eli, she smiled. Maybe he was just the hope she'd been needing. Maybe this attraction wasn't dead, after all, even though time and hard life lessons had kept them apart.

Nora didn't want to get her hopes up, but she couldn't deny she still felt that stirring in her gut whenever Eli was around. And from the way he looked at her, cared for her, she knew the attraction wasn't one-sided.

So what would they do about it?

Chapter Eight

Listening to Nora declare her marriage wasn't all she'd wanted was like a punch to the gut. He'd heard Todd say things about Nora back home, but Eli assumed that was just Todd talking through depression of being in the war.

Eli knew Todd's secret, but he'd always assumed that at home Todd and Nora were happy—because Nora was in the dark, mostly. Wasn't this baby proof of their wedded bliss?

"I didn't mean to upset you," he told her. "I guess I just assumed you and Todd had a good marriage."

"We did...at first." She let go of his hands to swipe at her damp face. "But we grew apart, out of love—if we ever truly loved each other beyond friendship. It happens. I would've stayed with him because it was the right thing to do. I mean, he was off fighting for our country and had a great deal of stress. I think the love just wasn't there. We were better at being friends than playing house."

And war would test even the strongest of relationships. Eli had hated hearing about Todd's time with Nora over the past few years, but what could he say? Eli had walked away from the woman who would've spent her life with him. So all the torture had been his own fault.

"He did love you," Eli stated. It was so important that she knew because Eli never doubted that Todd loved Nora; he just happened to love another woman, too. A secret Nora could never know. "He talked about you all the time, so don't doubt it."

Eli may have fudged the truth a tad, but he didn't want Nora's memories of her late husband to be tainted or for her to feel guilty for the marriage that wasn't everything she wanted, everything she deserved.

Nora smiled. "Thank you for telling me."

Gripping her hands again, he pulled her to her feet. "I know it's late, but I have an idea."

Nora laughed. "You've got that look in your eyes."

"What look?"

"The one that says you're up to something. Remember, I knew you and your brothers when you were troublemakers. I know when you're plotting."

Eli shrugged. "I'm older now and a little more reserved than I used to be."

Nora quirked a brow. "Reserved? The St. John boys are anything but reserved."

"Well, we're calmer now." He wrapped an arm around her shoulders and steered her toward the kitchen. "What do you say we make a batch of Snickerdoodles?"

Nora groaned. "You know my weakness."

"Hey, who said anything about you? I didn't have any dessert tonight and I can't remember the last time I had homemade Snickerdoodles."

Smacking his chest playfully, Nora laughed again. Music to his ears. Anything he could do to keep her smiling and not living in the past full of heartache was worth it. Besides, he still wanted an excuse to be with her, to talk to her, look at her. He'd missed so much time with her because he'd purposely distanced himself, but right now the last thing he wanted was distance.

He was torturing himself by spending all this time with her. But he could no more leave than he could stop this pull of renewed attraction toward her, and damn if that didn't complicate his life even further. He thought being back home would be fine, somewhat difficult but doable. He had no clue how fast and hard Nora would tumble back into his life in a fresh, new and terrifying manner.

In the process of making cookies, they moved around her kitchen, adding ingredients and working together. And by working together, they regressed to their youthful days by throwing flour at each other and making a pretty good mess.

"Now who's going to clean this up?" she asked, smiling as she glanced around the flour-covered countertops and wood floor.

Eli shrugged. "I'd say the same people who made the mess."

"Really?" The tone of her voice, the naughty grin she offered him, scared him…and completely turned him on.

Before he knew it, she'd taken an egg and smashed the shell overtop of his head. Yolk ran down the sides of his head and Eli couldn't help but laugh…and retaliate.

In an instant he'd cracked one atop her head, too, and she looked right up at him and laughed. Before he knew it they'd tossed more flour at each other, accidentally knocking the sugar canister to the floor. Kerfluffle darted through the room, glanced at the mess and darted back out.

When Nora started to back away from Eli, she slipped on the tiny granules. In one swift move, Eli grabbed her around her waist, hauling her up against his chest.

Her rounded belly bumped against his stomach. He loved the feel of her pregnant, loved how beautiful she looked growing with a child she already loved so much. No, the baby wasn't his, but the woman…

No, she wasn't his, either, no matter how he wished for different circumstances.

"You okay?" he asked, helping her upright.

Nodding, she kept her eyes locked on his. She

licked her lips and tried to push her egg-soaked hair from her face. "I guess we should start cleaning up."

He needed distance. She felt too good in his arms, smelling sweet and tempting just like he'd remembered. The playful way they clicked into place had even more memories rushing to the surface, threatening to take control over his common sense.

How could everything between them still feel so right after all these years? Shouldn't they feel awkward around each other as if trying to get to know each other again? Yes, they were totally different people, but that strong bond of friendship apparently tied them together no matter what had passed between them—time or marriage.

Every moment they were together they clicked on some level. Which just went to prove the bond they'd formed as teens was impenetrable. "Why don't you go shower? I'll clean up in here."

She tipped her head. "But you're a mess, too. I have a shower down here if you'd like to use it before we start cleaning."

Oh, no. No way could he shower in the same house knowing she was in the shower, too. Temptation was something he was taught to avoid and Nora threatened to drive him positively mad.

"I'll be fine," he assured her, fighting his innerdemon. "You go on. I'm sure there will be plenty for you to pick up when you're done."

She only hesitated a second before she nodded and left the room. Once he heard the bathroom door close upstairs, Eli rested his hands on the counter, the edges biting into his palms. With his head hanging between his shoulders, he let out a long breath.

While he didn't want to shower here, he did want the sticky, runny egg off his head and to take this breather to focus on rebuilding that wall of defense where Nora was concerned. He couldn't get wrapped up in her again. He knew his heart couldn't take another beating and walking away this time might be even worse than the last. He had a major promotion he'd been champing at the bit to get and Nora was expecting a baby. There was no way they could overcome all of that and attempt to rebuild anything stable.

After he grabbed the shampoo from the downstairs bathroom, washed his head in the sink and then toweled off, he went to work in the kitchen.

He found a broom and dustpan in the utility room off the kitchen. The sugar-flour mess on the floor was quickly cleaned up, as was the disaster on the countertop.

He'd just wet a rag to go over the stickiness on the counter when he heard Nora step into the kitchen.

"Wow, you made quick work of tidying up," she told him, glancing around the room.

But he didn't see anything but her, standing in a short, pale-blue fleece robe. The ties pulled together just above her rounded belly, showcasing the baby bump.

Even the little blue slippers on her feet were cute.

But it was the damp hair that hung in long, golden rope-like strands over one shoulder that drew him in. Her face was scrubbed clean and glowed with a soft pink tint.

She was everything he wasn't—everything he'd lived without for years. Soft, delicate, almost innocent in her own sweet way. He hadn't been lying the other day when he'd told her images, memories, of her is what got him through the hard times when he'd been overseas.

When her eyes landed on him, she froze. He couldn't do this. The ache he felt for her was too strong, too much to bear while trying to hold on to some type of sanity.

Eli crossed the room to her, watching her eyes widen. She tipped her head up to keep her eyes on his. As his body brushed against hers, Eli brought his hands up to frame her face.

"I can't lie to you, to myself," he whispered. "I need to touch you, Nora."

He didn't give her a chance to stop him. Another second without her would've destroyed him. Eli captured her lips with his, relieved when she opened, letting him in.

Delicate hands slid up his arms, then clutched at his shoulders. The familiar taste, the familiar touch, of Nora sent sensations shooting through his body that he hadn't felt since the last time he'd truly kissed her…and that peck the other day didn't count.

A slight moan escaped her as he changed directions of the kiss. His hands moved to the tie at the robe and quickly had it falling open. Sliding his hands up her sides, encountering silky material, only made her moan again. When he reached her breasts, she arched into him.

This is what he'd missed. Nora's instant response to his touch. Nora's vibrant passion.

Nora. All of her.

When he started to slide the straps of her nightgown aside, her hands came up to grip his wrists.

"Eli," she panted against his mouth. "We did this once. It didn't work and…I can't do heartache again."

Resting his forehead against hers, Eli closed his eyes and nodded. She was right. How could he be so selfish and try to take something she was probably willing to give, all the while knowing he'd walk away?

Hadn't her husband done the same thing? Sleep with her and then leave, whether for deployment or another woman's bed? Not that Eli would ever cheat on her.

Either way, Eli was no better because he was looking at the here and now instead of the future. A future for him and Nora simply didn't exist.

As he eased back, he pulled her robe closed and tied it back above her belly. Once he met her eyes, his heart clenched.

Sadness, regret, passion—they all stared back at him.

"This is hard for me," he admitted. "Being back here with you, discovering the woman you've become, makes me want more. This is so much different than before."

He cursed under his breath and scolded himself

for opening up too much. Letting that vulnerability seep out was a sure way to end up hurt.

Nora reached up, stroking his face with her delicate hand. "We each made choices of where we wanted to be, Eli."

"I hated being torn in two. When I left here…"

He shook his head, knowing he couldn't bare his heart too much more or he'd make an utter fool of himself.

"I'm selfish," he told her, cupping her hand beneath his. "But I can't think around you."

"I know," she whispered. "I feel it, too. I wish I didn't, but I do. This is a complication neither of us need right now."

He touched his lips slightly to hers once more because his willpower was pretty much nil around her. "I promise to be on my best behavior from now on."

Nora looked up at him and smiled, nearly melting him on the spot. "I've seen your best behavior, Eli. You'll have to try harder."

Smoothing her damp tendrils from her forehead, Eli kissed her there. "For you, anything."

Stepping back, he released her, hating the chill that enveloped him at the loss of her body's heat. "I'll be here Thursday to cook as promised. Saturday, if you don't have plans, I have a surprise for you."

"A surprise?" she asked, quirking a brow.

"A friend surprise," he corrected. "You in?"

"I'm a little scared of your surprises," she told him, crossing her arms over her chest. "I still remember that time you surprised me with a day at the lake, and when you talked me into skinny-dipping, your brothers had been hiding and they took my clothes. I still say you knew all about that."

Eli had honestly forgotten that time, but as the memory flooded to the surface, he burst out laughing. "I can admit now that I knew they were up to something, but I didn't think they'd take your clothes."

"Why didn't they take yours?" she asked, still smiling.

"They were teenage boys. They'd much rather see you naked than me."

Biting her lip to suppress her grin, Nora nodded. "Well, as long as my Saturday surprise is nothing like that, then I'd be happy to free up my day for you."

Warmth spread through him and he seriously felt like the nerd in school getting asked to the prom by the head cheerleader. Only this was Nora, and she was so much more than anything he'd ever been rewarded with.

"Great. I'll be here tomorrow and dinner will be ready when you get home."

She moved across the room and pulled out a drawer. "Here," she said, holding a key out to him. "This is a spare. If you're going to cook, you might as well keep it."

A key to the kingdom…for a princess he didn't deserve.

"I'll see you tomorrow."

Grabbing his coat and leaving out the back door, Eli hurried home. The blast of cold air didn't do a thing to help the heat spiraling through him after having his mouth, his hands, on Nora.

No more. He couldn't do that to either of them again. He was only teasing himself into thinking he could have anything with her now. And she certainly had enough on her plate without worrying about him pawing at her again.

Tomorrow when he cooked for her, he'd be just her friend. Even if it killed him.

Chapter Nine

Saturday morning came with beautiful sunshine, melting some of the accumulated snow. Of course, when the temps dropped again tonight all that melting would be in vain as the watery mixture turned to ice. Strange weather for this small town, but she was actually enjoying the extra layer of wintery ambience for the Christmas season.

Nora couldn't wait to see what Eli had in store for her today. And, as promised, he'd been the perfect gentleman the other night when he'd prepared dinner for her. So what did he have planned that was such a surprise?

She slid her feet into her knee boots and grabbed her purse. She assumed casual was the way to go since he was picking her up at ten in the morning.

What on earth could he have planned? Hopefully not too much alone time because the other night in her kitchen nearly caused her to cross every boundary she'd put up for herself. The way his hands had slid inside her robe as his mouth assaulted hers—the image they made kept rolling through her mind, arousing her even more.

Nora knew with certainty that the emotions she felt toward Eli had nothing to do with old memories jumbling up her mind. She was starting to have very strong feelings for the man he was now, the man who dropped everything to take over his father's practice for a few months, the man who made sure to check in on her. He'd done so much with his life, just like he'd wanted, yet here he was putting that life on hold to care for those he loved.

And she knew he loved her, even if just on a friendship level. Eli loved her just as she did him. But they couldn't cross over into the intimate territory. Never again.

As she came down the steps, her doorbell rang. Through the sidelight she could see more than one person.

Had he planned a party?

Crap. A party. She still hadn't talked to him about an anniversary party for his parents. She seriously had to do that soon. Days were slipping away so fast lately.

When she opened the door and saw Bev standing beside him, Nora couldn't help but smile. "Okay, now you've got me intrigued."

"What would you say to going shopping for baby furniture?" he asked with a wide grin. "My treat. No arguing. It's my gift to you and the baby, but I figured you'd want a woman's perspective so I brought Mom along. Drake is babysitting dad for a few hours before his shift."

Joy filled her and Nora had no clue how to even respond to such a generous gift. "I don't know what to say," she told him.

Bev reached out, patted Nora's arm. "You say thank you and hop in the truck."

Laughing, Nora met Eli's dark eyes. "Thank you. You have no idea how much this means to me."

As much as she wanted to refuse such an overwhelming offer, Nora knew she'd be a fool to turn him down. Besides, Eli had gone to the trouble of getting someone to sit with his father and asking his mother to come. He obviously wanted to do this.

But was the gesture out of guilt or pity? Part of her wondered, but the other part of her prayed Eli's kindness came out of their years of friendship. Actually, if his actions stemmed from anything akin to what they shared in her kitchen the other night, that was definitely not pity.

When they arrived at the store, Bev walked on ahead and Eli waited on Nora. Wet snow had started earlier in the morning and Nora's foot slid on the pavement as she started to get out of the car.

"Easy," he said, grabbing her elbow to assist. "Let me hold on to you until you get inside."

"You're not holding on to your mother."

Eli laughed. "My mother isn't pregnant."

Nora laid a hand on his arm and stopped just inside the entrance to the store. "I meant what I said earlier, Eli. You have no idea how much this means to me."

The tenderness in his eyes melted her heart. "I know what this means to you, Nora. I also know you'd never ask for help or let anyone know what you need. I don't want you to worry about cost. Go get whatever you want for your baby girl."

Unable to resist the moment, she reached out, wrapping her arms around his waist. "I don't know what I did to deserve you in my life," she whispered, trying to hold back the tears that seemed to accompany breathing lately. One day she'd break. An emotional meltdown was inevitable at this point.

"I'm the lucky one, Nora."

His soft voice murmured against her ear, sending shivers down her spine. Another time, another place, flashed in her mind of him holding her, whispering promises of forever. But that was a lifetime and plenty of heartache ago.

Eli pulled back, smiled and tugged on her hand. "Come on. I'm sure Mom already has a buggy full of frilly things by now. We'd better get in there and control her."

Eli stood back and examined all the pieces scattered across the hardwood floor. There was a reason he wasn't an architect or engineer. He was used to fixing people, not inanimate objects.

He refused to be intimidated by something as simple as a baby crib. He had a PhD, for crying out loud. How could he not understand these directions written in plain English?

"What are you doing?"

He turned toward the door where Nora stood, arms crossed over her rounded belly.

"I'm putting the crib together."

"Eli, you bought everything I'd ever need. I didn't expect you to put the crib together."

With her scrubs on and her hair pulled back in a low bun, she looked adorable…as usual. Lately everything about her set off some level of hormones with him.

"Not that I'm not grateful, but isn't this your night to cook?" she asked, a smile flirting over her unpainted lips.

"It's in the Crock-Pot. I put it on at Mom's this morning and brought it over after work so I could concentrate on this crib."

"Why don't you leave it and let's go eat."

He glanced at the neatly separated piles of various sizes of screws, slats and bolts. The directions—printed in what he was sure was three-point font—crinkled in his hands and he tossed it down.

"You're right. This could be a while and I need sustenance."

Before he could walk out, Nora laid a hand on his arm and looked up at him. That gentle touch never failed to send a high dose of sensations through him. Nora may be delicate, but she held all the power where he was concerned.

He'd still not gotten that very heated kiss and make-out session out of his head. How could he go on like he hadn't tasted her, felt her? Nora was a very passionate woman and he wanted to rediscover that passion more than anything.

But this was not his place. Another man later down the road would steal her heart and Eli would have to stand back and watch.

"Please don't feel like you need to do everything, Eli." Her big blue eyes studied him. "I know Todd was your friend, but that doesn't mean you have to take over where he left off."

Eli gripped Nora's shoulders, easing his face closer to hers. "You think I'm doing this for Todd? I'm doing this for you, because I care about you."

Nora shook her head. "Eli—"

"No, Nora." He made sure to keep his touch light, even though he wanted to shake some sense in her. "Everything I do for you is because I can't stand back and *not* do it. I can't help the feelings I have for you. I've tried to ignore them, but…damn it, Nora, I can't."

Her mouth parted as she gasped. "You can't have feelings for me, Eli. If you do, they're just old ones."

Taking his hands and framing her face, Eli stroked her jawline. "These aren't old feelings."

Her lids dipped down for a moment before she met his gaze again. "There's too much I want, Eli. Too much that you can't give, and right now I have to concentrate on this baby and the very real possibility of moving. I can't face these emotions I have for you."

The selfish side of him was thrilled she'd admitted she actually had feelings for him. But the other side of him cursed himself for making her feel torn.

Eli placed a gentle kiss on her lips and rested his forehead against hers.

"Nora, I'm here. Whether you need a friend, or anything else, I don't want you to be afraid to come to me."

She nodded, gripping his wrists. "I've missed you, Eli."

That soft statement packed a punch right to his gut. Damn, he'd missed her, too. Missed her so much he'd been ready to forget reenlisting in the army, especially since he'd finished his degree. He'd been ready to come home and see if they still had a chance.

But then she and Todd had gotten married.

After the wedding, he'd been afraid to visit too often when he was actually in the States, been afraid he'd see all that he'd let go in order to travel the world and enjoy his freedom.

"Let's go get some dinner," he suggested, pulling away. "I'm going to need a supervisor, putting this crib together."

He linked his hand in hers and led her toward the kitchen. The seed had been planted. Nora was very well aware of where he stood right now, and if she wanted to do anything about it, the proverbial ball was in her court.

Eli didn't know what scared him more—if Nora didn't act on her feelings…or if she did.

Chapter Ten

Friday morning meant another week closer to getting back to Atlanta and another week closer to leaving Nora and her baby. In some weird, twisted way he'd come to think of himself as the expectant daddy. He'd felt the little life move beneath his palm, had put together the nursery furniture and had even helped Nora research diapers and formula.

And he'd found himself Christmas shopping for Nora after he'd gone home last night. A Christmas present, for pity's sake. He needed to chill out and stop letting his hormones override common sense.

Eli picked up the chart from the door holder and glanced at the name. With a sigh he pushed the door open, ready to get this day behind him because he had a terrible feeling he was coming down with something. The headache and sore throat were one thing, but he was worried he was running a low-grade fever.

"Maddie, how are you feeling today?" he asked as he entered the exam room.

The elderly woman, who'd now donned some type of velour zebra-striped sweat suit, merely shrugged her shoulders. "Not much different than when I was in here a couple weeks ago."

Eli set the file down on the edge of the counter and leaned back against the edge, crossing his arms over his chest. "So you're really just checking up on me?"

"Now, Eli, I have better things to do with my time than to check up on you." She pursed her bright red lips together and let out a big sigh. "I want you to look at my wrist."

His eyes darted down to her hands in her lap. "What did you do to your wrist?"

Shoving her sleeve partway up her forearm, she held out her frail-looking wrist for his inspection. "I was exercising on my pole and one hand slipped. I landed on this one."

Exercising on my pole were words he really didn't need to hear coming from a senior citizen who used to threaten his life with her rolling pin.

Eli examined her wrist, careful of his touch as he rotated it, had her wiggle her fingers and apply pressure to his.

"This looks like a sprain, but I'd like to send you over for an X-ray just in case. The swelling isn't too bad. Have you been putting ice on it?"

Maddie shook her head. "I didn't have time. I baked some bread for you before I came in."

Eli resisted the urge to groan because who knew what flavor she'd concocted this time. "You need to take care of yourself, Maddie."

Reaching over with her good hand, she took a loaf from her purse. "I hope you like pumpernickel banana. Until you tell me what you like, I'll keep making up my own blend."

Eli took the loaf, laughed and nodded. "Maddie, I won't be here long enough for you to worry about my favorite kind."

She harrumphed before taking her cane and sliding off the table. "I've heard you've been spending time at a certain vet's house."

Of course she'd heard. This town was too small, the people too nosy, for anything to remain private. Reason number four hundred and eighty-two for him to get back to Atlanta.

"Stonerock is an addicting town," she went on. "You're back now and I bet if you think about it, you'll agree that fate has handed you a second chance at where you should actually be."

Eli studied her. "Are you getting philosophical on me?"

"Just stating a fact. Your father will retire soon. This surgery might be just the eye-opener you both needed."

Eli wrote out her order for an X-ray and waited until she shuffled out of the room. He eyed the bread and started to toss it in the trash like he did the last one, but that seemed cruel.

The first time he'd been skeptical, but she was obviously extending the proverbial olive branch to him.

Still, pumpernickel and banana? He chuckled. He picked up the loaf and headed to the front desk where Lulu was typing away on the computer, doing actual work on insurance claims. He tossed the foil-wrapped surprise onto the desk and smiled.

"From Maddie."

Lulu glanced over at him, looking over the top of her rhinestone-rimmed glasses. "Oh, honey, I can't eat that. Too many carbs. I like to save my carbs for my margaritas."

Eli shrugged. "I won't eat it, either. Just the combination sounds disgusting."

Lulu took a sip from the plastic cup she'd brought from home. That cup was always on her desk and Eli knew his father had never asked what was in it—Eli flat out didn't want to know. But as flighty as she seemed with the whole bimbo facade going, she really did run this office smoothly. He didn't catch her working often, but everything was always done on time and in an orderly manner.

Lulu set her cup down and slid off her glasses as she smiled. "Maddie always brought your dad cinnamon raisin bread. You might as well tell her your favorite or she'll keep giving you odd mixtures for spite."

Eli laughed, shaking his head. "So she told me.

What's your favorite? I'll tell her that because I'm not sticking around long enough for it to matter."

"Give it to Sarah. That girl can use a few added pounds. But if Maddie can do a vodka-flavored bread, I'll take it." Lulu donned her sparkly glasses and went back to typing. "Such a shame you're not staying, though. I think you're fitting in nicely here."

No, he wasn't. He was merely filling in for his father and then Eli would be back to Atlanta, hopefully heading up the trauma unit. He couldn't wait.

As he walked back down the hall, Sarah had just put another file into the slot. "Rooms one and two have patients," the young girl told him.

"Thanks, Sarah."

His father's newest nurse was straight from school, quiet, and one rarely knew she was around. Quite the opposite from Lulu.

When Eli pulled the chart from the slot, he paused. Maybe he couldn't wait to get back to the job he'd trained for, but that meant leaving Nora…again. He'd known this would be hard, and that's the main reason he'd stayed out of her bed. Well, that and because she was beyond vulnerable.

Coughing into his arm, Eli flipped open the chart, recognizing the name of the elderly gentleman waiting on the other side of the door. That was something else he wouldn't have in Atlanta. He rarely knew a patient in a town of that size.

And that was how he liked it, right? Eli shook off the questions swirling around in his mind. He couldn't stay. It wasn't an option. That didn't mean he didn't care for Nora and her child, though.

Caring for someone didn't mean you had to give up your goals and forget everything you'd worked for. He could still care for her from a distance; they could still remain friends. And when the time came for her to remarry...

A heavy weight settled into his chest. The last thing Eli wanted was to see Nora fall in love and marry again. The first time had nearly killed him. But who was he to ask for more? The last thing she needed was for him to express that he may be falling for her again.

The sound that greeted Eli when he came in the door really made his day. Nora's laughter filtered through the house, as did that of his brother's. Lord help him, his mind immediately went back to when they were all teens.

After the morning with Maddie and her questionable bread, he'd treated three positive cases of the flu. That made ten total since he'd arrived home.

And he refused to believe his lethargic state had anything to do with that dreaded bug. He could not, would not, get sick. He'd actually tested himself before he left and the swab came back negative. Thank God.

This is precisely why he preferred traumas. Besides the fact the work environment was fast paced and ever changing, he wouldn't contract any and all viruses.

Still wearing his coat, Eli went into the family room in the back of the house. Nora's feet were propped up on Cam's lap and Eli had to clench his fists. They were friends, this meant nothing. Besides, what claim did Eli have over Nora? None whatsoever.

"That house is not even an option," Nora said, still laughing. "I can't believe the agent considered that one. Seriously?"

Eli leaned his shoulder against the doorframe. "You're already looking at another house?"

Nora snapped her head around and glanced up him, her smile still in place. "It's time I started."

"I just put that crib together the other day. Does that mean I'm going to have to disassemble it to get it out of the room?"

Her smile faded. "Well, I haven't found a house yet and I've no doubt this baby will come before I actually move."

"Eli, are you all right?" his mother asked from the other side of the room where she sat next to his father. "You seem...grouchy."

He raked a hand over his face. "I'm just... I'll be out in the apartment if anyone needs me."

The questioning gazes annoyed him. He hated the fact that he was obviously the mood spoiler, but seeing Nora so cozied up with his brother, plus the fact she was looking for another house when he knew damn well she loved the one she was in, just got to him. Besides, he'd told her he'd find a way to help her keep her house.

How many times over the years had Nora made

herself at home exactly like the scene he'd just witnessed? She truly was part of his family whether he was comfortable with it or not. Hell, she'd spent more time with his family in the past several years than he had.

Eli made his way out to the garage and up to the apartment. Obviously his father was being taken care of for the evening, but he'd check on his parents again before he turned in for the night. First things first, he needed to get something to eat. Maybe that would help him feel better. Eli moved through the open floor plan and into the kitchen. Before he could fully study the contents in his fridge, the garage door closed below and footsteps sounded on the stairs.

Watching the door to the living area, he wasn't at all surprised to see Nora step through the door. Worry filled her eyes as she stared across the room.

"Did you have a bad day?" she asked, still holding on to the doorknob and standing in the doorway as if she didn't know if she'd be invited in or not.

"Just busy. I didn't mean to snap at you. You're the last person I would ever be mean to." He rested his palms on the edge of the counter and dropped his head between his shoulders. "I was caught off guard with everyone here, more caught off guard that you'd gone and talked to a Realtor."

"I told you I needed to," she informed him.

"You love the house you're in," he told her, pushing off the counter and crossing the room. "I hate that you feel you need to move because you don't have Todd to help anymore."

Nora shrugged. "It's okay. Life happens and I just have to make the most of what I'm dealing with."

He took her hand off the knob and closed the door behind her. How easy would it be to throw away everything and just stay here with her? How easy would a life with this breath of fresh air be? But what right did he have to think he could be included in anything regarding her life? He'd thrown it away once before.

Nora reached up, touched his face and frowned. "Eli, you're pretty warm."

"I'm not feeling too good actually."

"Why didn't you say something sooner?" she demanded.

Eli shrugged and moved back into the kitchen. "It's no big deal."

"Get back in here and lie down. I'll make your dinner. And you're having soup."

Eli chuckled, heading back into the living area. "I'm not arguing."

Her hard gaze softened as she looked down at him. "Now I know you must feel bad."

Resting his head against the back of the couch, Eli groaned. "This isn't how this works. I'm the doctor."

"Looks like you're the patient to me."

Before she moved away, Eli grabbed her arm. "Go home, Nora. I can't let you catch whatever bug I've got. I tested negative for the flu earlier, but who knows what this is. Could just be a quick twenty-four-hour thing, but still. I won't be responsible for you getting sick."

"I'll wash my hands and make sure to stay back

from your face." Nora's beautiful smile spread across her face. "You honestly think I'm just going to leave you when you have no energy and you feel this bad? What kind of friend do you think I am?"

"The best kind."

Her eyes held his a little longer before she pulled from his grasp and went into the kitchen. If he'd felt better he would have ventured to explore the heat, the friction, that had been bouncing back and forth between them for weeks.

"You need to get out of all those layers and try to get that temp down," she called to him. Eli hated that she was right, but he was starting to shiver and the thought of taking any clothes off made him colder. But he had to get this fever down. Of all times to be sick, he couldn't afford to be out of commission now.

After shrugging out of his shirt, he toed off his shoes, letting them thump to the floor between the sofa and the small table. His jeans went next, leaving him in his black boxer briefs and socks. Not the way he'd imagined stripping down when being with Nora again.

"Do you even feel like eating?" she called from the kitchen. "Maybe just some crackers for now?"

"That might be best."

He heard her opening and closing cabinets, then the rattle of a bag. When she came around the couch to hand him the package, her eyes fixed on his bare chest.

"If I felt better I'd take you up on the offer of that look in your eyes," he muttered.

She thrust the crackers at him and quirked a brow. "If you felt better your shirt wouldn't be off."

Eli nibbled on a cracker, praying that he'd feel himself by morning. When Nora rustled around more in his kitchen, then in his bathroom, he wondered what she was doing, but she came back with some medicine and sat on the coffee table directly in front of him.

"Take this," she told him. "We need to get that fever down."

Feeling ridiculous shivering in his underwear and socks—could this moment get more humiliating?—he eyed her over the meds. "Please, Nora. Go on home. I'll take this, crawl into bed and hopefully sleep it off."

Her eyes narrowed. "You're sick."

"Which is precisely why you need to go."

"I've been in here for a half hour. If I'm going to get it, I've already contracted it. I promise I'll be fine."

On a groan, he closed his eyes and rested his head against the back of the sofa cushion. "I don't have the energy to argue."

He waited for her to go, waited to hear the door close, but silence enveloped him and, before long, he drifted off.

After Nora called to the main house and informed Bev that Eli was sick, Bev tried to get her to go home. No way. Right now all Nora cared about was Eli and taking care of him.

Her baby rolled and Nora froze. That was new.

Kicks here and there were becoming more and more common, but that felt like a flip. With her hand on the chair and another on her belly, Nora stood still and watched Eli sleep on the sofa. He was wiped out. Between taking care of her, his father, his father's practice, it was no wonder.

Guilt slid through her. She should've refused his help. All of his downtime had been spent with her or his father. He needed time for himself, but having him around brought out the selfish side of her. She wanted to be with him all the time, wanted to talk to him, make new memories with him.

Eli had zero intention of staying, yet she found herself wondering, wishing. And she didn't have those teenage dreams in her mind like before. Now she knew full well that the chances of them being together were slim to none. That wouldn't stop her from enjoying him while he was here.

When Nora was sure her daughter was finished working on her Olympic routine, she crossed the space between her and Eli and felt his head. His fever was coming down. A sheen of perspiration covered him from the breaking fever.

As a concerned friend, she couldn't take her eyes off him. She wanted to be here if he needed anything when he woke.

But as a woman, she couldn't help but admire his chiseled physique. He'd been a muscular guy in school, always lifting weights with his brothers, always tinkering with cars. But now as a man those shoulders had nearly doubled in size. Taut skin stretched over rippling muscles across his back, shoulders and arms. A tattoo on his back curved up over his shoulder and she knew it went around to the front of his pec. He hadn't had that when he'd left town at eighteen.

He hadn't had that scar across his brow and down onto his cheek, either. That was very new because he'd been home for a visit a year ago and she hadn't seen it.

So much had happened to him since he left. A lifetime, really. But the man who had come home, the man she was now caring for, was taking her heart again and there was no way she could stop him.

Nora shoved her hair out of her face and sighed. She had no place in his life, no reason to know what happened when he'd been overseas fighting for their country.

Knowing he'd been hurt bothered her in more ways than one. She hated the thought of him being injured, but more than that she hated she wasn't part of his life enough to know, enough to show him she cared.

So here she sat, pregnant with her late husband's baby, falling for her first love all over again and scared to death of the future. She was a mess.

Yawning, Nora crossed the room to turn on a small lamp. After turning off all the other lights, she moved to the bed, which was on the far wall. The open floor plan worked to her advantage because she could lie there and still see him and hear if he woke and needed anything.

The garage light outside illuminated the window on the opposite wall. Snow started falling again. Being stuck in Eli's apartment on a cold winter night was not a bad place to be. She only wished she could be in his room, in his bed, under different conditions.

Unable to resist, she snuggled her head deeper into his pillow, inhaling his strong, masculine scent. Was she wrong in not resisting her feelings toward Eli? Because, as the days went on, her feelings for him deepened.

Tears pricked her eyes. Damn it. She didn't even know what to feel anymore. If she could have anything she wanted, she'd take Eli back into her life, and they'd fall in love and live happily ever after. But that wasn't reality and Nora would do good to remember that.

Closing her eyes, she allowed the tears to flow. She hated crying, hated the vulnerability that overcame her. More than anything she hated letting anyone else see her as anything but strong.

She knew this moment would come, when she'd be unable to hold back the dam of emotions. Maybe she needed to let go. Getting rid of all the angst, the worry, the fear she'd kept bottled up for so long was long overdue.

Once she cried herself to the point of a headache, Nora wiped her damp face and pushed back her hair. Eli needed her and that's what she would focus on. She had no choice but to be strong just a bit longer around him. She didn't want him to see her visibly upset because he had some guilt that seemed to shadow him at all times.

And Nora had a feeling that guilt stemmed from something she knew nothing about.

Chapter Eleven

Eli shifted, rolled over and opened his eyes. Blinking twice he focused on the beauty in his bed. That vision could cure any ailment.

With her blond hair spread around the pillow, *his* pillow, and her delicate hand beneath her cheek, Nora even slept like an angel. How long had his guardian been keeping watch over him?

Eli sat up and the room spun just a bit. Lethargy and an empty stomach were definitely things he could handle. Thankfully his fever was gone.

More than once he thought he woke to someone stroking a cold cloth across his head, his chest. Now he knew for a fact someone had and that someone was Nora. She'd sacrificed herself again and he didn't deserve her undying loyalty.

Todd hadn't deserved it, either.

Nora was a true gem and, in Eli's opinion, better than anybody. But she needed to get out of here. She needed to start keeping her distance because, God help him, he wanted more. He wanted her, and the sight of her tangled in his sheets only solidified the ache, the want.

After he carefully walked to the bathroom and gave himself a few minutes to freshen up so he didn't look like death warmed over, he went back into the living area and crossed to the bed.

Easing down on the edge of the mattress, Eli laid a hand on Nora's delicate shoulder. A very unlady-like snore filled the silence and Eli couldn't help but smile. She'd die if she knew she sounded like a farm animal. And even that tiny imperfection only made her that much more adorable.

Damn it. Now he was thinking of terms like *adorable*. His brothers would punch him in the face if they knew.

Eli slid his free hand over the scar above his eye. Wouldn't be the first time he'd gotten into a fight where this woman was concerned…and he'd do it again in a second to defend her.

Glancing at the clock, he was surprised to see it was almost noon. Thankfully it was Saturday.

"Nora," he said softly.

She stirred, her lids blinking open. She looked across the room, then up to him. In a second she sat straight up and put a hand to his face.

"Eli, are you all right? Why are you up?" She

scrambled to get the sheet from her waist. "You should've yelled for me. I didn't mean to sleep so long."

Eli placed both hands on her shoulders, easing her back down on the bed. "Calm down, Nora. I'm just fine."

Her brows drew together as she reached up to feel his forehead. "Your fever is gone. Thank God. I was hoping those cold cloths and the meds would help. But how do you feel?"

"When a man wakes up to a beautiful woman in his bed, he feels pretty damn good."

Nora rolled her eyes. "I'm serious."

"Me, too."

"Well, you must feel fine since you're hitting on me." She started to get up, but Eli placed a hand on either side of her hips, trapping her beneath the sheet. "Why the hurry?"

"Because…well, just because."

Rendering her speechless was quite a compliment. Eli smiled. "How are you feeling? Baby still moving okay?"

Nora nodded. "She's pretty active."

Eli wanted to feel the baby, wanted to lay his hand on her stomach, but what right did he have? This wasn't his child, wasn't his woman. But a part of him wished desperately that both belonged to him.

He was nervous for Nora, nervous for a healthy baby to come into this world. Damn it, he'd even bought the baby a Christmas present even though she wouldn't be here in time for Christmas. He couldn't stop himself when he'd seen the little purple stuffed elephant in the grocery store the other day. One minute he'd been getting milk and bread and the next he found himself in the baby aisle looking over everything from wipes to puff snacks. Then a small section of plush toys had caught his eye and the purple elephant had ended up in his cart.

He was a total goner and he hadn't even met the baby yet.

With her eyes locked on to his, Nora eased up the hem of her sweatshirt and placed his hand against her warm abdomen. The slight movement had him spreading his fingers, wanting to feel more, wanting to hold this moment forever.

Resting her hand over his, Nora's smile spread across her face, her eyes lit up. "I never get tired of feeling her move."

Guilt slid through Eli as he slid his hand away and came to his feet. Damn it. He couldn't get more entangled. He already wanted too much.

"Something wrong?" she asked, her eyes meeting his as she tugged her shirt down. "I just assumed you didn't mind, but I know some guys are grossed out by pregnant women."

"Those guys are idiots," he told her, rubbing a hand over the back of his neck. "I love feeling your baby, Nora. I just… Damn it, Todd should be here. He should be the one experiencing this. I feel like I'm invading his space."

Nora shoved her hair back away from her face, untangled herself from the sheet and eased back against the headboard. "You're not invading his space, Eli. To be honest, if he were still alive, I don't even know that we'd be together."

Shock rippled through him. Surely she didn't know. Waiting to see how much information she let out would be best. God knew he didn't want to hurt her any more than she'd already been.

"Why wouldn't you be?" he asked.

Nora toyed with the stitching on the edge of the old quilt on the bed. "We weren't like most married couples," she whispered. "The love…it just wasn't there. Not the way a husband and wife should love each other. I loved him as a friend and he felt the same with me, though neither of us quite came out and said it that way."

Eli eased back down on the edge of the bed and laid a hand on her leg. What could he say? She sounded so vulnerable, so torn. Empty words wouldn't help, wouldn't repair the broken marriage or bring Todd back.

"When he came home the last time I was determined to fight for our marriage." Her eyes came up to meet his. "I only planned on marrying once, having one family with one man. I wanted that security, that bond."

Yeah, he knew all about that stability she'd craved. Never once in her life had she had someone to fully depend on. Everyone had left her—from her parents, to Todd…to him. He was just as guilty.

"So I tried to do everything for him when he came home," she went on. "I made his favorite meals, seduced him trying to build a romance…but I could feel him slipping away. I blamed the army. I can't imagine what you guys see, what you all do, when you're gone. I wanted him to know I was here for him no matter what. But a piece of him was missing and he wasn't even acting like my friend anymore."

Eli clenched his fists, hating how broken she sounded. Those unshed tears in her eyes pierced his heart, which was nothing less than what he deserved.

"I found out he'd died on a Thursday," she whispered. "Friday I was served divorce papers and on the morning of the funeral two weeks later I discovered I was pregnant."

Eli had no words. Divorce papers? Todd had never mentioned that. Had he really planned on divorcing her and he never mentioned it? Instead, he'd come home on leave, slept with her and left without a single word.

Eli's anger for his late friend sent rage through him. What the hell kind of coward did that?

But then reality set in. Those divorce papers had to be partly Eli's fault. The fight he and Todd had gotten into, the one and only time they'd thrown fists at each other, had been over Todd's infidelity. Eli hadn't been able to stand it any longer. Nora had deserved better and Todd got angry when Eli called him on the matter.

But this was the first he'd heard of divorce papers.

His eyes focused back in on Nora as she wiped a single tear slipping down her cheek. The woman had always been so strong, so proud, heaven forbid people see her as human.

Eli reached out, grabbing her hands in his. "Nora, Todd and I did see some ugly things. It's a whole different world over there, a world I'm sure he didn't want to talk about with you because he was only here for a short time. I truly had no clue about the divorce papers. He never said anything to me."

"I wondered." She looked down at their clasped hands. "I was so embarrassed when I got them. That sounds selfish and cruel, but I couldn't believe it. I was still in shock over his death, but then to have those come, I just…I never thought he'd actually leave me. Especially without talking to me about it."

Yeah, that was something Eli couldn't believe, either. But there was nothing he could do about Todd's choices now, nothing he could do to ease her pain. Sometimes life experiences sucked and only time could heal them.

Eli cupped her chin, raising her gaze to meet his. "You were an amazing wife. Todd was lucky to have you. Maybe he felt you shouldn't have to put up with a husband who was always gone or maybe he was dealing with so much… Hell, I don't know. I just know I don't want you blaming yourself."

"Who else would be to blame?" she asked.

Stroking his thumb along her jawline, Eli stared into her damp eyes and knew he couldn't tell her the real reason she wasn't to blame. She was already hurting, why add to it? Why tell her Todd was sleeping around? That time had come and gone and Nora was trying to rebuild her life, her future, with her baby.

He wished he could give her everything she'd ever wanted. Nora should have the world handed to her because she'd been through an insane amount of heartache in her life. And yet she kept fighting.

"You're going to be an amazing mother," he told her.

A slight smile formed across her lips. "I hope so."

As her eyes continued to hold his, sadness and worry slowly turned into something else…something more heated and curious. Those baby blues darted to his mouth, then back up to his eyes.

She could tempt the strongest of saints. Unfortunately, where Nora was concerned, he wasn't strong at all and he sure as hell had never been a saint.

With his hand still cupped beneath her chin, Eli eased forward, closing the gap between them and claiming her lips. She parted for him, slowly sliding her tongue across his, slowly torturing him with her softness, her sweetness.

Over the past several years he'd been hardened from all he'd seen and taken part in. But right now, with Nora's delicate touch, he knew she deserved someone who could be gentle, patient. The hurt in her would take time to heal, and while he may want to be that man, in reality that was impossible. Even though she had moved on from her failed marriage with Todd, Eli didn't deserve her, either.

Yet he didn't back away.

Placing both hands on the sides of her face, he

shifted his body and eased her down onto his bed. Nora's hands slid over his bare shoulders and into his hair.

Those delicate fingertips left gooseflesh in their path. The swell of her breasts, the slight bump in her abdomen, felt perfectly right tucked against him. Everything about Nora in his bed felt perfectly right.

Except the fact she shouldn't settle and he wasn't staying.

Allowing himself another second of bliss, Eli finally eased back, then rested his forehead against hers.

"Nora, we can't do this."

Her hands came to curl around his shoulders. "I know."

"It's so hard to resist you. So hard when I want you more than my next breath."

"I understand."

Eli doubted it, but he sat up, trying to keep his eyes off her swollen lips, her tousled hair and how damn good she looked spread out on his sheets.

"We need to get out of here before I totally forget I'm trying to be a gentleman."

"I'll just head on home." She eased her legs around him and stood. "I'm really glad you're feeling better, Eli."

He watched as she headed to the door to get on her shoes. When she reached up for her coat, Eli crossed the room in two strides and gripped her arm, turning her to face him.

"Since we both have the rest of the day off, I have an idea," he told her. "What do you say?"

"What's the idea?"

"I'm not telling. Are you in or not?"

Her eyes narrowed as she bit her lip, then she finally nodded. "Okay, but I at least have to change and you...well, you need to be wearing more than boxers and socks."

"Deal." Eli laughed. "Let me grab a quick shower and check on Mom and Dad. I'll be at your house in thirty minutes. Oh, and dress warm."

As soon as she left, Eli's eyes traveled back to the bed. Getting her out of that had been the smartest move he'd made—the hardest move, but still his smartest.

Shaking his head as he moved toward his bathroom, Eli figured up the time he had left in Stonerock. On one hand, he couldn't leave soon enough. On the other, the thought of leaving clenched his heart. He'd never been ready to stay in one place before.

Unfortunately, now he had two places he wanted to be.

Nora had no clue where they were going. The silence in the car was deafening and Eli's fresh-from-the-shower aroma enveloped her.

That intense moment on his bed really had her thinking...as if she'd been able to concentrate on much else other than this man lately.

As they passed all of the neighborhoods and turned

to head into town, Nora wondered what he had in mind. She had a pretty good idea.

"You sure you're feeling better?" she asked.

"Promise. There's no way I'd be out with you if I thought I'd get you sick." He reached over, grabbed her hand and squeezed. "I'm still upset you stayed and put yourself at risk, but if the roles were reversed, I would've done the same."

Nora smiled. "Is that your way of saying thank you?"

"Yes. You were there when I needed you."

But where were you when I needed you? She wanted to ask, but let the moment pass. Rehashing the past over and over would get them nowhere and, to be honest, she didn't want to live in the past. She totally loved the Eli she used to know, but this Eli was different. There was almost a vulnerability to him. He'd seen and done more in his life than she'd ever know, which added a layer of intrigue.

The new Eli who greeted her nearly every day had her thinking of the future, thinking of them in ways she probably shouldn't.

He captured her attention and touched her deeper than he ever had before. And even though he was leaving soon, he was here now and she'd take every second with him and turn it into a blessed memory.

When Eli turned into the park entrance, Nora smiled. Talk about a memory. They'd shared many here.

"This okay?" he asked, turning to look at her.

"More than okay. I haven't been here forever."

"Seriously?"

Nora stared at the light dusting of snow covering the fountain in the middle of the entrance, the evergreen wreaths on the gates. "I never take the time to come. Occasionally I'll walk a few of the long-term boarding dogs, but I tend to just do that on the street by my clinic."

"Well, then, we'll just have to make the most of it today."

Giddy with excitement, Nora jumped from Eli's truck and pulled her hat down farther over her ears. Even the chill in the air couldn't ruin this moment.

When he came around the side of the truck and took her hand, Nora accepted it and let him lead her through the entrance. Since it was nearing evening, some families were out showing kids the Christmas displays set up around the park. A small makeshift cabin posed as Santa's toy shop, an old red caboose was adorned with a festive garland and a Santa was actually standing at the railing taking pictures with a line of children.

Nora's free hand went to her belly as she thought of her baby girl. This time next year she'd be in that line waiting for precious milestone pictures.

Eli's hand squeezed hers. "I can already see you dressing up your little girl for her first photo with Santa."

Smiling up at him, Nora nodded. "I can't wait."

They walked on, heading toward the arched stone bridge that crossed over the wide creek running through the park. Nora stopped on the bridge, resting her hands on the concrete barrier.

"I've always loved this spot the most," she told him, looking down at the water, outlined by snow.

Eli leaned down, wrapped his arm around her waist and pulled her against his side. "I know. You told me you wanted to get married in this park, right here on the bridge."

Shocked, Nora turned her head to look up at him. "You remember that?"

That had always been her idea of a dream wedding, but dreams obviously change.

"I assumed you and Todd would marry here."

Nora shook her head. "I would've, but he was being deployed soon so we just went to the courthouse."

The muscle in Eli's jaw ticked and Nora looked back down to the water.

"You've had to give up so much," he murmured. "And you still find the positive outcome in everything."

"I learned long ago there's always someone with bigger problems than me. In the grand scheme of things, I don't have many problems. I'm healthy, my baby is healthy."

Eli's hand on her waist slid slightly around to rest on the side of her belly. The warmth from his touch reached through all the layers and she loved the strength he possessed.

"Sometimes I wish I'd never left you."

Nora froze, turning her body and resting her bottom on the bridge railing. Looking down to her brown gloves, she stared at the creases in the leather, focusing on anything other than his admission.

"When I first left I questioned myself every single day," he went on, still staring out across the creek. "My first deployment helped keep my mind off you, but then Todd started talking about you and I knew the two of you had started something. I tried to tell myself that was for the best, that you'd moved on and you deserved to be happy. I knew after he got out he planned on living in Stonerock."

Nora bit her lip, saddened by the pain lacing his voice.

"But I hated every time he would mention your name as if you belonged to him. Because in my mind, you were still mine."

Nora's heart literally ached. "We'll always share a bond, Eli. You were my first love."

He turned his face toward hers, shifted his body and braced a hand on either side of her hips. "You were my first love, too, Nora. A love I'm finding may have never left me."

Before she could react or question his bombshell, his cool lips slid over hers gently, slowly, as if getting to know her all over again, as if they weren't familiar.

Nora held on to his thick arms, trying to steady herself as his gentleness overtook her. Had he just declared his love?

Pressing her hands against his chest, she eased back. "Eli, you can't spring things like that on me."

His eyes met hers. "I know, but I can't keep it inside, either, Nora. It is what it is."

"That's it?" She waited until another young couple walked by. "You kiss me, you say you love me, but you do nothing about it."

"Because this point in our lives isn't good for me to act on my feelings. I'm only here for a short time. What good would come of moving forward?"

Nora closed her eyes, drew in a deep breath and prayed for courage, prayed for surviving the heartache that would inevitably come. "Please, don't say things to me that will only hurt. I can't handle them."

When Eli's hands framed her face, Nora opened her eyes and took in his tortured look. Didn't they both have broken hearts brought on by no one other than themselves?

"I don't say things to hurt you. I say them because I know you feel this, too."

Why lie? There was no getting away from this discussion or these emotions.

"I do," she whispered. "I've tried to ignore the fact that every time I'm around you I'm happier. I don't want to depend on anyone again. I can't."

Because in the end they all leave.

"I'm not asking you to depend on me," he told her. "Maybe…maybe I'm asking if I can lean on you while I'm here. I need you in my life, Nora."

"As what, Eli? Your friend…or more?"

It was naive of her to hold out hope. She swallowed.

"Are you staying?" she asked, almost afraid of the answer.

Eli closed his eyes, sighed and shook his head before lifting his lids and meeting her gaze again. "Honestly, Nora, right now I'm not sure what I'm doing. All I know is that when I'm with you I have all these feelings…"

He pushed off and turned from her. Nora wasn't sure what to say, afraid that any words might ruin the moment, might ruin the sliver of a chance they still had. How long had she been hanging on to that sliver and not even known it?

A family walked through, the mom pushing a stroller and the dad with a little boy atop his shoulders. An ache in Nora's chest pulled her from the moment. A family is all she'd ever wanted. A stable family, a simple home, a loving husband and kids that would cause chaos.

Eli turned back to her, took her hand and started walking. Silence settled between them and she truly had no clue what shaky ground they'd just landed on, but she had a feeling they were just at the beginning of whatever journey fate had planned for them.

Eli stopped at a vendor selling hot chocolate and got two, handing a warm, steaming cup to her.

"I'm sure the baby will love the sugar jolt," he joked as he sipped from his cup.

Nora was about to respond when a horse and carriage went by. Smiling, Nora glanced at Eli.

"Come on," he said, taking her free hand. "No need to give me the puppy-dog eyes."

Nora laughed as Eli led her to the park information area. In no time they were climbing on board their very own white carriage with red velvet seats. An oversize black fur blanket awaited them and Eli was quick to settle it across their laps.

"Good evening," their driver called over his shoulder. "Just sit back and enjoy the ride."

Eli's arm came around her shoulders and Nora snuggled against his warm side. She would most definitely enjoy the ride. How could she feel anything but excitement and anticipation now that Eli had revealed his feelings? But apparently he waged an inner war with himself over the matter.

There was so much about this man that contradicted the life she wanted, the family she longed for.

He'd seen things she couldn't even imagine, had lived on his own for so long. He made a life when he left here, a life that didn't include her. Had he really reconsidered?

"I can hear you thinking," he whispered in her ear. "Relax."

Nora's baby kicked and squirmed a bit, a sensation Nora never grew tired of. She placed her gloved hands over her coat and waited for more. This was the life she'd dreamed of years ago, a wintery carriage ride through the park with Eli, a family of their own...

But this family wasn't theirs.

Nora closed her eyes and settled her head on Eli's shoulder. How could she deny herself when this may be the second chance they both deserved?

Chapter Twelve

Nora flipped her sign to Closed and sagged back against the door. She'd sent her receptionist home early and stayed behind for the scheduled pickups and emergencies, but this was her late night and her feet were killing her.

At least her ankles hadn't started swelling yet. At what point in the pregnancy would that blessed event take place? Thankfully the nausea had stopped a week or so ago—an early Christmas present from God.

Her belly growled and Nora knew the peanut butter and crackers she'd snacked on all day had gone directly to the baby. Flipping the lights off as she moved through the office, Nora's mind drifted to her house where Eli would be cooking for her. She loved the one night a week he'd taken it upon himself to be her personal chef. What woman wouldn't want that?

Milo, one of the dogs currently boarded, darted between her feet and Nora had to grab on to the wall to keep from tripping. "You silly pup. Come on in the back."

She took him to his room where he stayed at night and gave him his favorite treat. "See you in the morning," she told him with a kiss to his wet nose.

Nora grabbed her purse and keys, set the alarm—an insisted-upon early Christmas present from Mac and Bev—and headed out the back door. She hated leaving when it was dark, especially since the break-in, but the sun set so early in the winter, she really had little choice in the matter.

As she settled into her car, her cell rang. Cameron's name lit up the screen.

"Hey, Cam," she greeted as she pulled from the lot. "What's up?"

"Just wanted to follow up with the break-in. Are you busy?"

"Actually, I just left." She maneuvered her Jeep through the snow-lined streets. "Did you come up with anything?"

"I wanted to let you know that I have another case I'm working on and I'm pretty sure the two are tied together. I can't tell you more, but you are safe and I seriously doubt they'll be back."

Worry for her friend slid through her. "You okay, Cam? You sound… I don't know. Tired."

"That's exactly what Megan just told me," he said

of his best friend. His humorless laugh filled the line. "I'm fine, Nora. I just wanted to give you peace of mind. I'm trying to close this case as soon as possible, but it's taking longer than I thought."

"That's what makes you an awesome chief. You take your time and cover all your bases."

"More like other people's bases," he muttered.

Nora knew he protected people for a living, but she'd also heard he sometimes protected those he believed in, helping them get back on the right track. Cam wasn't just a cop; he was a man of dignity and one who genuinely cared about people.

"You headed home?" he asked.

"Yeah. Almost there."

"Tell Eli I won't be around for a few days."

Her worry deepened as she turned onto her street. "Want me to tell him more?"

"No. Work-related and I can't discuss it. I already talked to Mom and Dad, but I didn't want him to worry. I'll be out of commission with my cell for a while."

"Just stay safe," she told him as she pulled into her drive, smiling at the sight of Eli on a ladder stringing lights above her porch. "Call me when you can and let me know you're okay."

"I will. Love you, Nora."

"Love you, too, Cam."

She disconnected the call, but couldn't help the fear she had for her friend. Even in this small town there was crime and he carried the entire weight of each incident on his shoulders. Nora knew his friend

Megan worried just like they all did. But Nora had a hunch Megan's feelings for Cameron extended beyond friendship.

Nora stepped from her car and walked toward the porch. "You cook, you decorate… Tell me again why you're still single?"

Eli laughed, looking down from the ladder. "Because there's only one woman I would let catch me."

Okay, well, that wasn't subtle.

"What made you decide to put up lights?" she asked as she pulled her coat over her ever-growing belly.

Eli slid another bracket onto her gutter and hung another strand. "I know how much you love Christmas and your house is the only naked one on the block. Besides, I think I was driving dad crazy."

Nora laughed. "Maybe because you two are so much alike. What did you do now?"

Eli climbed down the ladder and moved it a few feet over. "He keeps quizzing me on his patients and I don't know how many times I've assured him I have not driven any of them away."

"He's worried. He can't help it."

Eli threw her a look over his shoulder. "He threatened to have Mom bring him so he could sit and monitor."

Holding back her smile, Nora shrugged. "He's bored, Eli. He's in the house all day, and he's still in pain from the surgery. Maybe he *should* come and sit for an hour or so. Patients would love to see him and he'd feel better."

"I'm not a damn kid," he all but growled. "I know what I'm doing."

Nora refused to answer his mumbling, defensive tone. Those two St. John men couldn't be more alike...no wonder they butted heads more often than not.

"Go on in," he called down as he hung up another clip. "I'm almost done and there's chili on the stove. Corn bread is wrapped up in a pan."

Nora went inside, taking in the spicy aroma of the chili. She turned her tree lights on in the living room and smiled. Next year she'd have an extra stocking hanging by the fire place, cute little "Baby's First Christmas" ornaments on the tree and a reason to "believe" in Santa again.

There was just something about a baby that made life seem so innocent and simple.

Nora shrugged out of her coat and hung it by the door. Tugging off her gloves and hat she hung them up, too.

She'd just finished her bowl of chili when Eli came stomping up the back steps. Nora went to open the door for him and was greeted with a blast of arctic air.

"You really didn't have to freeze just to put lights up for me, you know."

He pulled off his black knit hat. "I was trying to get them done before you got home, but I ran late at the clinic today and then the whole dad thing."

Nora sat her bowl in the sink and turned to lean against the counter, her arms crossed over her belly. "Did you eat?"

"Yeah, right before I went outside."

"Oh, Cam called when I was on my way home. He's going to be out of commission for a few days. He said he already talked to your mom and dad, but he didn't want you worrying."

Eli nodded, shoving his hands in his pockets. "He's working on a big case. I have no clue what. Even Megan doesn't have a clue and he tells her everything."

Yeah, Megan was his best friend since grade school. Those two were as close as siblings, but he always confided in her before anyone else, which really worried Nora.

"He sounded so tired."

"He's a big boy," Eli told her. "He'll be fine. But whatever he's working on is taking a toll on him."

Crossing the room, Eli came to stand right in front of her, placing his hands on her shoulders. "How are you doing? Is work getting too much for you?"

"Not yet," she assured him, loving the feel of the weight of his hands. "I'm actually taking a half day tomorrow because I have a doctor's appointment and then I'm running by my Realtor's office to see a couple of listings she printed off for me."

Eli frowned. "Do you love this house?"

Yes, she did. But being a single mother taking care of a home this size, the financial burden and the memories were all driving her out.

"I'll love a different house," she told him with a smile.

"Answer my question. Do you love this one?"

She looked directly into his eyes and nodded. "Yes."

"Then let me help you figure out a way to stay here."

He was asking as a friend who cared for her, so she smiled. "Fine, but I need to at least have plan B in place in case we *can't* figure it out."

"I'll agree to that." His warm smile spread across his face as he dropped his hands from her shoulders. "I want to come with you."

"Which place?"

He smoothed her hair behind her ears and rubbed his hands down her arms. "The doctor's appointment and the real estate office."

"You already closed early the day my office got broken into. If you cut out early again your dad will most definitely set up camp there to make sure you're doing things the right way."

Eli laughed. "Don't even give him the idea."

"Listen, it's just a regular checkup. I'm not having an ultrasound or anything."

Eli drew his brows together and sighed. "Fine. I just hate you doing this alone."

She reached out, wrapped her arms around his waist and settled her cheek against his warm sweatshirt. "I'm not alone. I have you and your entire family. I couldn't be alone if I wanted to."

His hands came up to cup her face, turning her to meet his gaze. "Is that what you want? To be alone?"

The way his husky voice filled the room seemed

to make that innocent question take on a whole new meaning.

Nora shrugged. "I've been alone most of my life. Even when I lived with my mother she was hardly around. Then when I graduated she moved, you went into the army and your parents let me live in the apartment over your garage. I dated, but never found someone until Todd. Then he was always deployed and now…I guess I don't know any other way."

Eli's strong hands stroked her face as he took another half step toward her, closing any gap that had been between them.

Nora swallowed as his dark blue eyes bore into hers. "Maybe I'm tired of being alone, too," he murmured. "Maybe, just for tonight, we should take what we want, what we've been dancing around since I came back."

Nora closed her eyes, afraid to take in the meaning of his proposal, afraid she'd want so much more than what he was offering…but more afraid he'd see just how much she wanted him.

His warm breath tickled her face, his body shifted against hers, and even with her eyes closed, she knew he was moving in to kiss her. Parting her lips, she waited until his tongue skimmed her mouth. Gentle at first, Eli took his time as he continued to hold her face between his firm hands.

Nora slid her arms up over his shoulders, locking her hands behind his neck and toying with the ends of his wavy hair. Her baby moved, kicked a couple times, and Eli eased back.

"She kicked me," he muttered against her lips.

"I'm not at my most attractive state right now," she defended.

Eli's hands moved from her face down to cup the sides of her belly. "You're beautiful, Nora. You're the sexiest woman I've ever known, pregnant or not."

She loved how his hands felt on her stomach while the baby moved around. He made her feel attractive, wanted and cherished.

Nora placed her fingers on his chest, not to push him away, but to feel the strength, the warmth, of the man she craved and ached for.

"I can't deny I want you," she told him. "But are you sure? I mean…"

His brows drew together. "What?"

"I'm more concerned how you'll feel once you see me…you know."

Shame had her dropping her head between her shoulders. Eli's fingertips went to the hem of her scrub top and pulled it up. Then he went to work on the long-sleeved tee she still wore. Not wasting any time, he tugged it up and over her head, tossing it to the side, as well.

Nora refused to meet his gaze. How ridiculous she must look standing in her kitchen wearing black scrub bottoms, tennis shoes and a very unflattering white cotton bra that was barely containing her ever-growing chest.

When his hands slid up over her rounded stomach, Nora closed her eyes, suppressing a shudder. Chills danced across her exposed skin in the path his hands took. The tips of his fingers glided over the tops of her breasts and traveled around to the back to unhook her bra. Nora extended her arms, allowing him to remove the unwanted garment.

"Look at me," he demanded in a firm yet soft tone. "Don't hide from me, Nora. Ever."

When she looked into his eyes, she saw nothing but raw desire, a need she was sure matched her own.

"If you're unsure, tell me now," he muttered as his lips traveled over her bare shoulder, up the side of her neck and to the corner of her mouth. "Tell me I should go and I will."

As if she could speak at all now that he'd assaulted all of her senses. No way could she deny him or herself this pleasure they both so desperately needed, ached for.

Her arms came up around his neck as she eased back and looked him in the eyes. "I think we need to get out of this room, considering my curtains over the sink are open."

A smile played at the corners of his mouth. "I have no intention of sharing you with anyone."

He bent down and scooped her up with an arm behind her back and another behind her knees.

"Oh, Eli, you're going to hurt yourself. Put me down."

"You're still light, Nora."

He carried her with ease up the stairs and down the darkened hallway into her room where her small bedside lamp was on.

The fact he wasn't out of breath after carrying her

up a flight of steps spoke volumes for his strength and made him all the more appealing…as if he wasn't enough already.

When he eased her to sit on the edge of the bed, he stood back and stared down at her. Shivers of arousal threaded through her as his eyes raked over her body.

No way could she turn down this man. She loved him, had possibly never stopped loving him, on a level that terrified her. But she had to take a risk; she had to show him just how she felt because the words just wouldn't come…and she wasn't altogether sure he was ready to hear them.

"I've never wanted anything more in my life than the way I want you right now," he told her.

Suddenly feeling brave, Nora stared up at him and smiled. "Then take me."

Chapter Thirteen

As much as Eli wanted Nora, he also had a bundle of nerves to contend with. He knew Nora was riding a roller coaster of emotions regarding so much in her life. For tonight, though, he only wanted her to think about this, about them.

Eli stripped down to everything but his boxer briefs. A burst of arousal consumed him as Nora sat motionless and watched him the entire time, those bright eyes traveling over his body. That woman was more potent than any drug he'd ever administered.

He stepped between her spread legs and took her face in his hands, easing down to kiss her. She parted for him, her tongue dancing with his as he tried to force himself to go slow.

When he broke the kiss, she moaned. "Easy," he

told her, placing his hands on her shoulders and easing her back onto the bed. "You're still overdressed."

He removed her shoes and socks, then quickly got rid of her pants and underwear. Lying spread out on her bed looking all lush and sexy was making him crazy…and fulfilling every fantasy.

He quickly pulled protection from his wallet and readied himself before focusing his attention back on Nora. As always, the sight of her stole his breath, made everything else dim in comparison.

"The way you look at me…"

His eyes held hers. "How do I look at you?"

"Like nothing else in the world matters to you."

"Nothing else does matter, Nora." He brought his knee up on the bed and slid his body down beside hers. "Just us, here and now."

He couldn't look beyond right now because the possibility of leaving her nearly crippled him, but the idea of staying made him feel trapped.

As his hands explored her body, a body he hadn't touched in over a decade, he allowed himself the luxury of taking his time. They weren't teens trying to sneak around; they had nowhere else to be. And as much as he wanted to rush and take everything she was offering, he knew she deserved better. *They* deserved better.

As the darkness filtered through her windows, the small lamp cut a soft glow through the room. Her sweet floral aroma surrounded him, pulling him deeper into her world.

Carefully, he settled between her thighs. When

she reached out to him, Eli took her hands and placed them on his chest.

"Love me," she whispered.

"I do, Nora. God help me, but I do."

When he entered her, Eli closed his eyes, trying to freeze this moment when everything in his life was perfect. He'd finally come home. Her body shifted, but her eyes remained locked on him. The desire, passion and underlying vulnerability all looked back at him and Eli knew he'd die before he ever hurt this woman again.

When she cried out her release, Eli followed. And when the quiet surrounded them, he pulled her comforter around them and offered her a shoulder to sleep on, praying this wasn't just a one-time thing. He wanted more…especially now that his heart had just become fully invested.

She hadn't heard from Eli the entire day. Nora realized he was busy, but she'd sort of hoped after last night that maybe he'd reach out even if just through a text.

She killed her engine and stared up at the twinkling lights stretching across the roof over her porch. What they shared hadn't just been a one-night stand; there had been too many emotions, too much communication through locked gazes and lingering touches.

If all of that weren't enough to have her confused about where they were heading, he'd confessed he loved her. Yes, they'd been in bed and usually all verbiage there could be taken with a proverbial grain of salt, but there was no way Eli was just saying empty words. When he'd said he loved her, he'd sounded so torn, so full of conviction.

Carefully exiting her car, Nora went around to the trunk and popped the lid. After reaching in to retrieve the groceries, she wrestled the plastic bags up her arm, fighting them when they caught on her bulky coat sleeve. Between the doctor and the Realtor, today hadn't gone nearly as well as she'd hoped…

She sighed as she slammed her trunk. Just as she turned, she lost her footing. Groceries slid from her arm and onto the driveway, but Nora managed to save herself by clutching onto the spoiler on the trunk lid.

Seriously? Could this day get worse? All she wanted to do was go inside and put her feet up…per doctor's orders. Yeah, like bed rest was even possible. She had clients who depended on her. Not to mention, her bank depended on her, too, to make the mortgage payment.

She honestly wanted to sit and cry into her bowl of Rocky Road, but she didn't even have the energy for that right now. As she stared at the groceries lying in the driveway, Nora started laughing. Shaking her head, she stared up at the darkened sky. Sometimes you just had to laugh at all the obstacles life threw at you.

The tightening in her stomach had Nora leaving her groceries and heading inside. Her toilet paper and canned soup weren't going anywhere and there was no way she was going to bend over and haul those sacks inside. Nothing was worth putting her baby at risk for.

As soon as she let herself inside, Kerfluffle darted to the back room. Apparently Nora wasn't getting any sympathy from her spoiled cat. Fine.

After hanging her coat and scarf up by the door, Nora pulled off her boots and padded over the cool hardwood floor into her living room. She'd just sat on the sofa and pulled a throw off the back when her front door flew open, letting in another blast of cold air.

Eli's eyes locked on hers as he stared into the living area. "Are you okay?" he asked, closing the gap between them in about two strides. His eyes raked over her, his brows drawn down in worry.

"I'm fine, why?"

"You have groceries in the driveway and I thought something happened to you."

He had to be worried; he'd used the front door and everything. Nora rested her head against the back of the cushions. "At ease, soldier. I'm fine. I slipped in the driveway and had a little discomfort in my stomach so I left my stuff out there."

"Define discomfort," he told her, easing down onto the coffee table in front of her sofa.

Nora shrugged. "Some cramping and such."

Eli sighed, glanced up to the ceiling and shook his head. "I'm going to get your groceries. Anything in your car you need?"

"No."

Great. They'd entered awkward territory.

Nora settled farther into the corner of the couch and wrapped the blanket up around her shoulders. The cramping slid around into her back and Nora knew this was what her doctor had referred to as Braxton-Hicks contractions—more like the mother of all period cramps.

As she breathed through the pain, Eli shuffled back in the house. She heard him putting things away in the kitchen, then the bathroom, and by the time he'd come back into the living room her pain was under control.

He stood above her, staring down as if he wanted her to say something. She merely quirked a brow. "Yes?" she asked.

"Am I invited to stay?"

"Of course."

He picked up her feet and took a seat on the end of the couch, resting them on his lap. "Do you want to talk about your doctor's appointment and the meeting with your Realtor or do you want to discuss last night?"

She held his gaze, refusing to be embarrassed about last night and the fact it was the best of her life. And she wasn't quite ready to tell him about the whole bed rest thing or he'd turn all mother hen on her.

"I'd prefer to discuss last night, considering you left without telling me goodbye somewhere around midnight."

His eyes widened. "I thought you were sleeping."

"Would you have said anything had you known I was awake?"

Eli shifted his body so his hand rested on her shins. "Of course, Nora. I meant everything I said last night."

The intensity of his stare had her shifting herself. How could he have so much power over her? He consumed her in so many ways and she feared she'd start down this path to unknown territory with him only to be stranded in the end again.

"Are you sorry last night happened?" he asked, still studying her.

"No." She answered without hesitation because that was certainly one thing she was absolutely sure of. "I wanted you, Eli. I don't regret it."

"I'm sorry if you thought I just abandoned you, but I decided to head home so we could both sleep and be rested for work." His hand massaged her leg through the blanket. "Had I stayed, I only would've wanted you again."

Thrills shot through her at the fact he wanted her still. Before she could respond, another cramp settled like a band wrapping around her entire abdomen. She gasped and closed her eyes, waiting for the moment to pass quickly like all the others.

"Nora?" Alarm laced Eli's voice. "What is it?"

"Just a little cramping." She let out a deep breath and opened her eyes, meeting his worried gaze. "It's okay. I've been having them since this morning."

"What did your doctor say?"

Nora bit her lip and shrugged. "The baby is healthy. Her heart rate is right where it should be and she's measuring right on target for the due date."

"What aren't you telling me?"

He always knew when she was lying or holding something back. Everything with him always circled back to that unbreakable bond they shared…and the new one they'd formed.

"She put me on bed rest until Monday."

"Were you going to tell me that?"

"I just did."

Eli narrowed his eyes. "After I pried it out of you. Seriously, Nora, it's okay to lean on people. You're obviously going to need help for the next five days."

She groaned and dropped her head back on the cushion. "I don't have time for this. I need to work to pay my bills. This is ridiculous."

"Have you found a replacement for when you take maternity leave?"

Nora shook her head. "I know a guy who works a couple towns over. He did mention he could help out a few days a week. I was hoping to find someone full-time, but I may have to settle for him. At least I trust him."

"Then see if he can fill in for you until Tuesday."

Rubbing her belly, Nora nodded. "I already sent him a message. I'm waiting to hear back."

"I take it you didn't make it to the Realtor?"

"No."

"Good. I'm still trying to figure out a way to keep the house. Just don't make any decisions without talking to me first. Promise?"

Nora knew arguing was a moot point, so she simply nodded.

When Eli's fingers started kneading one of her feet, Nora couldn't hold back the groan that escaped her. When was the last time anyone gave her a foot massage?

Silence enveloped them and Nora had to fight to stay awake. The fact she could relax around Eli and let her worries go really spoke volumes for how much she cared for him. She'd never been this at ease with anyone.

Oh, she'd loved Todd as a friend and had trusted him, but there was always something missing. Her heart had always felt a void.

"I'll have Drake swing by during the day to check on you," he told her.

Nora lifted one lid. "I'll be fine, Eli. I can take care of myself. I'll just be lazy, sit here on my couch and watch home improvement shows all day."

"Someone will be checking on you," he insisted.

Loving his protective instinct and hating his no-room-for-argument tone at the same time, Nora sighed and focused her full attention on him.

"Listen, you all have enough going on with your dad and your work schedules. The doctor didn't say I couldn't fix myself food or walk around. I'm just supposed to take it easy because my blood pressure was high and I have some swelling." She held his gaze, noting the muscle ticking in his jaw. "Besides, if you hadn't come back I'd still be in this situation and I'd be taking care of myself, anyway."

Eli leaned across her legs, keeping his eyes locked

on hers. "But I am back and I am going to take care of you. Try to keep me out and I'll use my key."

Nora laughed. "I knew that would come back to bite me in the butt."

His hands rubbed her legs as he returned her smile. This is what she craved, the simple pleasure of being snuggled on the couch, talking with the one you loved. Of course she could do without the bed rest part, but still. Is this how things would've been had she and Eli never broken up?

More than once she regretted not following him, but she just couldn't. She'd been shuffled around so much in life that when she'd come to Stonerock, she'd fallen in love with the old-fashioned town with no stoplights and cute little shops lining Main Street and the people who welcomed her with open arms, continuing to love her after her mother had moved on once again.

"I'll get you something to eat," Eli offered. "Any requests?"

"Your night to cook is tomorrow."

He shifted out from under her feet and settled them back on the couch. "I think I can handle a can of soup or a sandwich for now."

"Anything is fine. Surprise me."

Before he walked from the room, Eli braced one hand on the back of the couch and touched the side of her face with the other. She had no choice but to look up at him, no choice but to see the love in his eyes. But how long would that last?

"We'll get through all of this, Nora," he whispered. "I won't let you be alone."

His lips slid over hers softly, gently, and then he was gone. Even the briefest of touches had her body responding and wanting more.

He promised he'd help her through "this," but did he mean these next few days or life in general? Because as much as she knew he cared for her she also knew Stonerock wasn't a place he wanted to stay. He had a fulfilling life in Atlanta.

No, she knew Eli well enough to know he was torn between the two places. But she couldn't beg him to stay, and she didn't want him to out of obligation. All she could do was offer support, to show him how much she loved him and let him make the decision that was best.

Nora rubbed her belly and feared the decision would be the same as the last time they were together. She'd told herself this time would be different. This time she'd be ready.

Truth was, she would never be ready to say goodbye to the man she loved.

Chapter Fourteen

"I promised, Nora. If I leave, Eli will not be happy and then he'll just take off and come here himself, then Dad won't be happy. You don't want to upset Dad, do you?"

Nora rolled her eyes. "Drake, you don't play fair."

The sexy fireman shrugged and offered that killer smile that most women swooned over. But to Nora, Drake was more like a brother than anything.

"I'm not playing," he told her as he took a seat in the oversize chair next to the sofa. "I plan on doing a little work while I'm here."

Nora adjusted her laptop on her legs and crossed her arms over her belly. "Really? What are you working on?"

"I have a couple of schools that are waiting for an

opening for a field trip, I need to look at switching some guys on the schedule who have conflicts and I need to talk to the mayor about funding."

Guilt washed through Nora. "Drake, please, go into work. I am perfectly fine."

Those dark blue eyes pierced her from across the room as he remained silent and raised one dark brow.

Nora held up her hands, silently admitting defeat. As she got back to her computer, where she was looking up baby name meanings, she barely heard him on the phone working.

So many names were beautiful, but Nora wanted that perfect one. There had to be one that would stand out above all the others, but so far nothing really pulled at her.

Since baby names weren't cutting it, she opted to search for homes in the area for sale. She wasn't making a rash decision, as she'd promised Eli, but she did want to know what was in her price range.

Lost in the house-hunting process, her ears perked up when Drake muttered Andrea's name. Andrea was his fiancée who'd died a little over a year ago in a tragic car accident where Drake had been the driver. Whoever he was talking to must've brought up her name. Drake was getting much better at talking about the accident and he'd finally stopped blaming himself fully, though he was still justifiably upset.

When her doorbell rang, she jumped, a hand settling over her stomach.

"Expecting someone?" he asked.

"Nope."

She adjusted to look over her shoulder as Drake went to answer the door. Nora barely resisted the urge to groan when she saw Patty Morrow and her cat carrier.

"I need to see Dr. Nora."

Drake stood in the doorway, blocking the woman from entering. "She's on bed rest right now."

"But Mr. Bojangles has the sniffles."

"Who is Mr. Bojangles?" Drake asked.

Nora came to her feet. "It's her cat. Let her in, Drake, it's too cold out there."

Drake stepped back and threw a narrowed glance at Nora. "My brother will not be happy about this."

"Your brother is not my keeper," she whispered before turning her attention to Patty. "Bring Mr. Bojangles into the living room."

Kerfluffle pounced from the couch, arched her back and stretched, all while watching the newcomer suspiciously.

"Take Kerfluffle into the kitchen, please," she told Drake.

As Nora examined Patty's feline companion, she came to the conclusion she always did where her best customer was concerned—nothing was wrong.

"Patty, Mr. Bojangles looks perfect to me. I'm sure the cold weather may be annoying to him, but he really is a healthy kitty."

Patty nodded. "I just never know and I worry if I hear him breathing funny."

The middle-aged woman had no children and

housed as many as eight cats. She was in Nora's office at least once a week.

"How much do I owe you?" Patty offered, taking out her wallet.

"Nothing," Nora assured her with a smile. "I'll be out of the office until Tuesday, so I'm sure I'll see you next week."

"Christmas is on Friday. Will you be out on Christmas Eve?"

Nora forced her smile to remain in place. "I'm sure I'll be in, just not sure how late that night."

After ushering the woman and her cat out the door, Nora went back to her post on the couch just as Drake came in with Kerfluffle.

"I don't know why you still let people come to your house," he muttered, handing Kerfluffle over.

Nora stroked her cat as she curled up in her lap. "It's a small town, everyone knows where I live. I can't tell them to quit showing up, that would be rude. Besides, it's not that often and I kind of like knowing I'm needed."

Drake picked up the remote and clicked on the television. "You'll be needed a hell of a lot more once this baby comes."

Elation spread through her. "I can't wait."

Drake propped his feet up on the ottoman that matched her oversize chair and tapped the remote on his leg. "You're going to be a great mother, Nora. I can't wait to see the little one."

Nora started to tear up; she couldn't help it. The thought of her baby actually being loved and held by everyone who meant so much to Nora just consumed her. She couldn't help but wonder if she'd look like Todd with his black hair and dark eyes or if she'd have her blond hair and light eyes.

"Oh, no. Please, if you cry Eli will definitely kill me."

Nora laughed and swiped at her face. "Trust me, he knows all about these pregnancy hormones. He's experienced them."

Resting his elbow on the arm of the chair, Drake smiled. "You and my brother have gotten pretty close since he's been home."

"We have a history," she said with a shrug. "I don't really know what we're doing, to be honest."

"He's never gotten over you, Nora." All serious now, Drake held her gaze. "When he left, he never planned on coming back, but then he got the itch to become a doctor and went to medical school. After that, I think he was coming back home."

This was all news to Nora. "Why did he reenlist again?"

Drake shrugged. "Not sure, really. He just told Mom and Dad that he'd changed his mind."

Why didn't she know he'd mentioned coming home after medical school? Not once had he reached out to her during that time. Had he come home years ago, would they have gotten back together? Would she have ever started talking to Todd?

Before she could question him further, her doorbell rang again.

"If that's another crazy cat lady..." Drake growled as he came to his feet.

"Excuse me? I'm a crazy cat lady, pal, so knock off the snarky comments."

He laughed as he passed by the couch and went to open the door. Nora glanced around again and smiled at the little redheaded boy who lived two doors down.

"Can I see Dr. Nora? My dog ate my mom's Christmas present."

Drake stepped back and laughed. "She's right in there, Brody."

As Brody approached, Kerfluffle darted off her lap and ran toward the Christmas tree in the corner where she started swatting at the ball of yarn ornament Nora hung there for her in hopes it would keep her from wandering through the tree.

The young boy with red curls poking out of his knit hat moved sheepishly through her house. "I'm sorry, Dr. Nora, but I started to wrap my mom's Christmas present—I got her some lotion at the Secret Santa shop at school—but when I went into my bedroom, Eddie was eating the bottle."

Nora patted his arm. "Puppies like to get into things. Is Eddie acting okay?"

Brody nodded. "He was sleeping on my bed when I left."

"I'm sure he'll be just fine. Why don't you give him some bread when you get home? The bread will help absorb the lotion. If he starts throwing up, that might be a good thing because he's getting it out of his system. But if he starts acting bad, like lying around and not being playful, call me."

Tears pricked Brody's eyes. "Will he be okay?"

Patting his sweet little face, Nora smiled. "With you watching over him, he'll be himself in no time. And I bet he'll really like getting bread instead of regular dog food."

Brody nodded. "Thanks, Dr. Nora. I'm sorry I bothered you at home."

"You can bother me anytime, Brody."

Drake remained at the door and let the young boy out. When he crossed back over into the living room, he shook his head and laughed.

"Don't say a word," Nora scolded. "He's the sweetest little boy. He came by a lot last year when his mom bought him a hamster. He was scared to death he'd hurt that thing. When it died, Brody brought him to me to see if there was anything I could do."

Drake settled in next to her on the sofa. "You're a bleeding heart, Doc."

"I'm happy to help my clients and their critters in any way I can. I love all living creatures."

Drake patted her leg. "Which is what will make you an amazing mother. You have this natural instinct to protect and nurture."

Nora smiled and yawned.

"You need to go lie down." He tilted his head and gestured toward the hall. "Go on. You might as well rest up now because when this baby comes, I'm guessing you'll be too busy for naps."

Nora laughed and swung her legs off the couch. "I'm just not good company."

As she came to her feet, Drake stood, too, and took her into his arms. Nora loved the St. John boys—all of them in different ways. She loved Drake for always knowing what to say, what to do and when to just be a good friend. Cam was impossible not to love with his mysterious, quiet ways. And Eli…well, Eli had a very special place in her heart that seemed to just keep growing with each passing day.

"I'm sorry I'm skipping out on you," she muttered into his chest.

"I didn't come over to be entertained, Nora," he told her as he rested his chin on her head. "I came over to be supportive. I'll be right here if you need me. Be sure to take your phone and, if you need something, just text me."

Nora pulled away and patted his stubbled face. "You're going to make an awesome husband one day."

A shadow passed through his eyes before he shot her a lopsided grin. "Let's not get carried away. I only show my soft side to you."

Nora headed to the downstairs spare bedroom because she just wasn't comfortable doing all those stairs when she was supposed to be taking it easy.

When she crossed into the bedroom with its cozy cream curtains and matching bedspread with pale yellow pillows, her eyes zeroed in on the box that had been delivered shortly after Todd's death.

A box of his belongings from the army. She'd put the box aside, not ready to dive into it when it had arrived. Considering the death, the divorce papers and the pregnancy, she just hadn't been ready for more emotional turmoil.

Should she look at it now? She was on bed rest for three more days so she certainly had the time. And if she wanted to even try to move forward with Eli, putting her past behind her was something she couldn't put off.

Nora sank onto the edge of her bed and sighed. Did she seriously think she could put the past behind her? That was a terrible, cruel saying.

Another cramp pulled at her abdomen. Nora eased down onto the bed and decided to rest for now. Worrying about the box and Eli's intentions wouldn't do this baby any good. But soon, very soon, she'd be tackling both.

Nothing could come between this baby and a healthy pregnancy and birth. Nora would do everything in her power to keep her child safe.

She pulled the cream comforter back and slid in between the cool sheets. All she wanted right now was some relaxation and rest. She had some serious life decisions to make and she needed to get them done fast because this baby would make an appearance in just over three months.

Chapter Fifteen

Eli looked over the incision on his father's leg from which they'd taken a vein and then he inspected the healing incision on his chest.

"Everything is looking good, Dad."

Mac pulled his sweatshirt back on and nodded. "I could've told you that."

Laughing, Eli put his hands on his hips and stared down at his father. "Yes, but you also told all of us that your chest pain had been indigestion and look where we are."

Mac grumbled, but Eli just ignored him. He'd had a light day at the office and he was anxious to get over to Nora's to check on her and relieve Drake.

His brother had already texted him and given a heads-up that a few of Nora's clients had stopped by for pet advice and that she was tired. He'd also said she'd been in the spare room for most of the evening, which troubled Eli a bit. Was she feeling worse and not saying anything or was she purposely avoiding the babysitter?

"Got a minute?" his father asked, easing back into his recliner.

Eli took a seat on the couch and rested his elbows on his knees. "What's up?"

"I'll cut straight to the point," his father said. "I'm going to retire soon. Very soon actually. I want to give you first dibs on my clinic."

Eli knew this day was fast approaching; he knew his father would offer and more than likely expect Eli to take over, but…

"I have a job, Dad."

"I figured that would be your answer had I offered a month ago, but since you've been back, you've been really close with Nora. I assumed you might have changed your mind."

Eli sighed, ran a hand over his hair. He didn't have a clue what he was doing. Yes, he loved Nora, now more than ever. He wanted to be with her, but he honestly didn't feel like she was in a place to make a big decision on her life, not when her husband was just killed a few months ago.

But the more he thought about staying here, staying with her, the more the idea appealed to him in ways he never thought possible.

"I'm not asking you to make a decision right now," his father went on. "But think about it."

Eli nodded. As if he could avoid it. He loved his family, loved Nora, but he had worked his butt off to become a trauma doctor and he had a good shot at this promotion. Did he really want to throw all of that away? Did he deserve another shot with her after he'd left once and still kept a secret about her marriage? What right did he have to take anything from her and pretend he was worthy of her love, of being in her baby's life?

For Nora he was about ready to do just that.

"I need to go check on Nora." Eli came to his feet. "She was put on bed rest and Drake was babysitting today."

"Is she okay?"

Eli nodded. "Yeah, just a precaution."

"Maybe you should bring her over here and we could be babysat together." Mac laughed.

He should've, but he assumed Nora wanted her privacy. After pulling his wool coat on, he went to the kitchen to kiss his mom on the cheek and headed out the back door. Once at Nora's he let himself in with his key and shook out of his coat. That wind was getting worse and another chance of snow was on the horizon. He was getting damn tired of freezing. This was Tennessee, for pity's sake, and this crazy weather was quite unusual.

Once he relieved Drake, Eli set out to the guest bedroom where she was resting. He didn't want to disturb her, but he needed to see that she was okay.

He looked in the doorway, saw her resting on her

side, the covers pulled up to her chin, and decided to pull the door just slightly.

Eli went into the kitchen to fix dinner while he waited for Nora to wake. He wanted to talk to her about her upcoming doctor's appointment and breaking news about his promotion.

On his way home, he'd been notified that the committee had narrowed down their choices to two candidates…and he was one of them.

Nora needed to know where he stood because he didn't want to lead her on, but then again, maybe he wasn't. What if he did stay? What if he took over his father's practice permanently?

He laughed as he pulled out a pan from beneath the stove. Was he really leaning toward staying in Stonerock?

Yes, he was. And to be honest, he'd been considering it since he realized he'd fallen in love with Nora all over again. He'd been ready to come back years ago before she married Todd, so why not now? How could he leave her knowing this second chance was practically his for the taking? That Nora was the only woman who would ever fill the void in his heart? He didn't have to let the past or Todd rule his future, not when being with Nora was just within his reach.

Eli started chopping onions and putting them into the pan to sauté. He added a drop of olive oil to the onions, sending them sizzling in the pan. Apparently he had more to talk to Nora about than he'd first thought. Now he couldn't wait for her to wake up.

A future with her…isn't that what he'd always

longed for? In all the places he'd been, with all the lives he'd saved, there had still been that piece missing from his life. But since he'd been back home, back in Nora's arms, he'd felt whole for the first time since he was eighteen years old.

Now he only hoped Nora was ready for him to be a part of her family, because he had no intention of going anywhere.

This may very well be the best Christmas ever.

Nora woke to a darkened room, only a soft glow from down the hall cut a narrow slant of light across the foot of her bed. A bit disoriented, she glanced at the clock. It was nearly eight. Good grief, she'd napped earlier when Drake was here, then had gotten up and gone back to bed because she was still exhausted. Being pregnant really messed up a body's system.

Or perhaps she'd just been going on autopilot for so long, since Todd's death, her body was finally just catching up.

She eyed the box next to the old antique dresser. The thought of digging into Todd's personal things gripped her heart. She wanted to know about his life away from her, but at the same time maybe she should just let it go. She'd buried him with honors and she had a baby coming to hold up his memory.

No, she owed it to her baby to face the truth. Her baby would ask questions one day and Nora needed to have the answers. But she couldn't go through the box now, not when she was still being babysat.

Perhaps once Eli went home to sleep…*if* he went home. He hadn't stayed last night, but he'd threatened to tonight. She'd insisted last night he go home, but she had a feeling he wouldn't let her get away with that again.

The scent of spaghetti sauce and bread drew her to the kitchen. She was positive her bedhead pony-tail had seen better times, like at eight this morning, but she figured her head warden had seen her at her worst, anyway.

When she stepped into the kitchen, Eli faced away from her, staring out the patio onto the dark-ened night.

"Penny for your thoughts?" she asked as she crossed to him.

Turning, Eli greeted her with a smile and opened his arms to take her in. "My thoughts were only on you. How are you feeling?" he asked, easing back to study her face.

"Refreshed." She laughed. "Poor Drake. I nearly slept the day away."

Eli shrugged and pulled her back against him. "Drake wasn't here for fun. He's fine."

Being in Eli's arms, having his strength surround her, had Nora wanting more. She didn't want him to leave, didn't want him to go back to Atlanta. But she couldn't ask him to stay. If she did, he'd only stay out of obligation and would regret his decision in no time.

"I made spaghetti if you're hungry."

Nora stepped away and made her way over to the stove. "The smell is what lured me in."

"And here I thought you came out to see me. You just using me for my cooking?"

She threw him a glance over her shoulder. "On Thursdays I am."

Eli clutched his chest. "I'm wounded."

He sat with her at the small breakfast nook while she ate and discussed her day of napping and caring for two patients. Once she was finished he quickly cleaned up the kitchen, after insisting she go lie down on the sofa. She conceded only because she loved having him in her home, taking charge and being all protective.

When he brought her in a bowl of Rocky Road ice cream, she nearly melted into a puddle of love right there.

"You've been such a good girl, listening to the doctor's orders, I thought you needed a reward."

Nora laughed as she took the bowl. "Whipped cream, too?"

He settled onto the couch next to her and propped his feet on the coffee table. "I stopped by the store on the way home. Figured you'd like some."

"You're so good to me."

She dove into the sugary mess and devoured every single bite.

Eli took her bowl back to the kitchen and Kerfluffle followed on his heels. When they returned, the kitty curled right up in Eli's lap.

"Looks like I'm not the only one who likes having you here," Nora said as she snuggled into Eli's side. "I really do appreciate everything you've done for me, Eli."

His arm wrapped around her and he kissed the top of her head. "If I didn't want to be here, Nora, I wouldn't be. But we need to talk about us."

Her heart nearly dropped. Those were words a woman never wanted to hear from the man she was in love with. "We need to talk" was just as bad as "it's not you, it's me."

"Don't tense up on me." He laughed. "I just think it's time we look at the big picture here, especially since we've gotten closer than either of us was prepared for."

He was right. They'd danced around the attraction for a while, but then spiraled straight into bed and into each other's hearts again without considering the long-term effects.

Nora sat up and turned to face him, drawing her knee up on the couch. "I know we didn't plan to sleep together. I told myself I wouldn't, that you would still be leaving and I would have to let you go."

Again. The word hovered in the air between them and she truly hadn't meant to blurt everything out, but if he wanted to talk, she needed to be honest and up front about her feelings and emotions.

Eli looked down at his lap as he stroked Kerfluffle. The muscle ticked in his jaw and he seemed to be contemplating what to say...or how delicate he should be with his words.

"Don't be afraid to tell me we can't have any more than just these few months together, Eli." She swallowed, forcing tears back as the ache in her body threatened to consume her. "I'm not eighteen anymore and I have a more realistic view on life. I didn't expect you to fall into bed with me and then fall in love all over again and decide to stay."

"But I have," he whispered.

Hope spiraled through her. Had she heard him right?

He brought his dark gaze up to meet hers. The intensity staring back at her had Nora's breath catching in her throat.

"I did fall in love with you again, Nora. I never stopped loving you."

"I know you said that the other night when…" She trailed off, shaking her head. "I just didn't know how strong you felt about me, about us."

He reached out, put one hand on her stomach and held her gaze. "When you say 'us,' I know you mean me and you. But when I say 'us,' I'm talking the three of us. I know this baby isn't mine, Nora, but I love you, and I love this child. I want to see if we can grow together, to be a family."

The tears Nora tried to hold back earlier came spilling down her cheeks…now for a whole different reason. He wasn't leaving her; he wanted to be with her.

"What about Atlanta?" she asked. "You loved being away from Stonerock."

"But I never loved being away from you," he told her. "I've been gone for years. Years. And in all that time I haven't found anything that comes close to fulfilling my heart the way you do."

Nora covered her face with her hands as sobs ripped through her.

"Oh, honey, please. Don't cry."

Eli's arms came around her and she found herself crushed against his chest.

"I know you've been on a roller coaster lately, so I want to take this slow." His soft chuckle vibrated against her. "As slow as we can considering we've already slept together. But I want to make this right and I don't want to mess this up."

Nora leaned back, swiping at her damp cheeks. "I'm sorry. I just… I thought you would never consider a life here in Stonerock, and then to hear you say you want to stay here, with me…"

She was at a total loss for words.

Eli's strong hands framed her face, his thumbs sliding away stray tears. "I'm staying here tonight. I'll stay every night if you let me."

She clutched at his wrists. "You can't stay tonight," she told him. "I can't… I mean, with the bed rest and the baby…"

"I don't expect to have sex, Nora." He kissed her softly. "I wouldn't do anything to jeopardize this baby or you. I want to stay because I want to feel you by my side. I want to wake up next to you before I go off to work."

"Why?" she asked, searching his eyes. "Why are you so intent on staying? I mean, there's only so much happiness love can supply. What about everything you've worked for?"

Eli shrugged, taking her hands in his and squeezing. "I'd been considering staying and Dad asked me if I'd be interested in taking over his practice. He wants to retire soon and I took his offering as another sign that being here was the right step at this chapter in my life."

"So you'll be the hometown doctor?" she asked with a grin. "Then we'll both have patients showing up at our door."

Laughing, Eli shrugged. "That's fine with me."

They watched a movie and when he started yawning Nora figured he needed some sleep. Just because she'd slept the day away didn't mean he'd had that luxury. He'd worked and had to get up tomorrow to work again.

"Why don't we head on to bed?" she suggested as the movie credits rolled.

"Sounds good to me." He came to his feet and helped her up. "But I want you in your bed. I'll carry you up."

Nora rolled her eyes. "You've got to stop carrying me. I'm getting heavier."

Without a word, he scooped her up, much like he had the other night, and carried her straight up the stairs and into her room.

As they readied for bed, Nora smiled. Is this what it would be like now that he was staying? He hadn't mentioned marriage, but he had to be heading in that direction.

Nora pulled her gown over her head as warmth spread through her. He was giving her time to come to terms with Todd's death and with the pregnancy. He was putting her and her baby's needs first and his last. How could she not be totally in love with a man like that?

As she sidled right up next to him beneath the crisp sheets, she inhaled his masculine scent and loved the fact that her bed now smelled of Eli. She wanted his presence to overtake this house, to fulfill her life as they both started forward on this journey.

Eli kissed her on the forehead. "This is the best part of my day. I love you, Nora."

"I love you, too," she whispered into the dark.

And she did. She loved this man with all of her heart, and she had to put her past to rest once and for all so she could fully invest in their future.

Tomorrow, she vowed, she'd go through that box.

Chapter Sixteen

He'd held her most of the night, he'd carried her down the stairs before he left for work and he allowed her the luxury of being alone with no babysitter if she promised to call at the first sign of trouble.

Nora really shouldn't like this whole alpha male routine, but she couldn't help it. She absolutely felt like she was everything to Eli, and because she was his world, she figured he wanted to protect her at all costs.

Her heart warmed at this new life.

But her past still shadowed her, and now that she was alone, it was time to tackle that.

She headed into the spare room and eyed the box in the corner. Nora slowly eased herself onto the floor beside the box and rested her hands on top. Once she opened it, all of Todd's military life would come spilling out—a life he'd purposely kept from her.

But by law those things were now hers.

Pulling at the edge of the packaging tape, she peeled it all away and pried back the flaps. She really didn't know what she expected, but right on top were his BDUs neatly folded. She pulled them out, hugged them to her chest and closed her eyes. The stories this uniform could tell...

After setting it aside, she reached in and grabbed an army-green bag. Opening it, she discovered a couple of books, his dog tags and a watch. One of the books slipped from her hands and a folded piece of paper slid out across the hardwood floor.

She reached for it and realized it was an envelope. When she flipped it over she saw it had been addressed...to her. The stamp was in the corner, but it had never been mailed.

Slowly she slid her fingernail along the seam and opened it up. Sliding out the trifold paper, Nora realized her hands were shaking.

The date at the top of the letter was dated two days before he died. Tears clogged her throat. He'd never sent her a handwritten letter while he'd been overseas. Emails, texts, phone calls, yes, but never a letter.

She rested her back against the dresser and began to read.

Nora,
I'm every kind of coward for writing this letter to you. I wanted so badly to tell you in person

when I was home on leave, but I just couldn't. You don't deserve this lifestyle or a marriage made to be spent alone.

I see how hard you work to make this marriage work, I see how you want this marriage to work, but I think we rushed into things and I know you don't really love me...not like a woman loves her husband. I realize you love me as a friend, and that's all I can ask for. You're the best friend I've ever had for putting up with me all this time, hoping our marriage would turn into something more.

But I have decided to file for divorce.

Nora swallowed. Well, at least he had tried to give her some sort of heads-up before the papers arrived. But he'd apparently put the plan in place long before he left to go back overseas.

She looked back down to his neat handwriting.

I hate to hurt you and if we stay married that's exactly what I'll continue to do. I've not been the best husband, Nora. I know you've been waiting on me back home. I know you've been praying for me, but I have not been as faithful to you. I had an affair. That's not easy for me to admit, nor is it something I'm proud of.

Nora read those last few sentences again, sure she'd read wrong. An affair? He'd cheated on her? Yes, they may have not had that level of love most men and women share, but Nora took her marriage vows very seriously.

Betrayal and hurt coursed through her.

But it was the next sentence that sliced her heart open. She read it twice; her heart beat harder and faster. Tears welled up in her eyes as she stared at the damning words through a blurry haze.

Everything she'd believed, everything she'd wanted for her future, her baby's future, was a lie.

Nora crumpled onto her side and clutched the letter to her chest. Sobs tore through her; an ache she hadn't experienced settled deep in her stomach.

Todd had died, leaving her alone with a baby. Eli had come back onto the scene, making her promises of love and a future.

But as of this moment, both men were out of her life. Both men had betrayed her and, according to the letter, Eli's betrayal was unforgivable.

Eli checked his watch at least six times in the past thirty minutes. He couldn't wait to finish his day and spend the weekend with Nora. They could work on the nursery, talk about the baby and just be together.

His nurse had placed the last client in room one and Eli pulled the chart from the holder. With a sigh and a smile, he opened the door.

"Maddie, it's good to see you this afternoon." He tossed the file onto the counter and washed his hands. "How's the wrist?"

Drying his hands, then tossing the paper into the trash, Eli rested his hip against the counter.

Maddie held up her hand. "Feeling better, though I'm still afraid to support myself on my pole. My workouts have gone to hell."

Eli couldn't suppress the grin. "I think it's wise to let it heal a bit more and I'm sure you can find another workout until then. Do you have a treadmill? You could walk. Just twenty minutes a day is good for you."

Beneath bright purple eye shadow, Maddie's eyes rolled. "Walking is just so…vanilla. I like a little spice in my life."

Spice in the life of a senior citizen is so not an area he wanted to get into…especially when it involved a pole.

Eli carefully checked out her wrist and requested she keep her splint on for another week. "Just come in between Christmas and the first of the year. I'm sure you'll be good to go then."

"I suppose I'll have to tough it out a few more days, then." She reached into her oversize bag again and pulled out another foil-wrapped loaf. "For the holidays I opted for peppermint berry bread."

Peppermint berry? Good heavens. Nothing about that sounded appealing…and how the hell did one make peppermint bread?

Eli took the loaf and laughed. "Cinnamon raisin."

Maddie quirked a brow.

"My favorite bread," he said with a grin. "It's cinnamon raisin, same as my dad. Looks like I'm staying and you might as well know."

Maddie slapped the paper-covered table. "Well,

hot damn, it's about time you came to your senses. Word around town has been that you're cozied back up with the sweet vet."

"Word would have this right. I plan on taking over Dad's practice and getting even cozier with the beautiful vet."

Maddie smiled, slid off the table and grabbed her rhinestone cane. "I'm glad to see she'll finally get a happy ending. That poor woman has really been through it."

Eli couldn't agree more. Nora was getting her happy ending…*they* were getting their happy ending, one long overdue.

"Have a Merry Christmas, Maddie."

She patted his cheek. "You, too, Doc."

Once she was gone he quickly closed things up and sent Lulu and Sarah home for the long weekend. He wanted to get out early and stop by to see a friend who could help him with a surprise for Nora.

Eli may be rushing things, but he had to let her know just how serious he was about her, about staying and starting a new life.

He only hoped his friend could keep things on the DL. It would be the ultimate Christmas surprise.

After he made the all-important stop, Eli made his way to Nora's. The twinkling lights across her porch called him. The tall tree in her wide window also twinkled and Eli couldn't wait to make this their home. Couldn't wait to start their life together the right way.

He let himself in the house and called out her

name. He didn't see her in the living room or kitchen. Maybe she'd decided to lie down. He went into the spare room she'd been resting in and found her lying on top of the cream comforter, a letter clutched to her chest. She was asleep.

Eli crept closer and nearly tripped over the box in the floor and the contents strewn around it.

His gut clenched. These were Todd's things. Nora had spent the day going through her late husband's belongings from overseas.

Eli's eyes darted back up to her and now he noticed the tear tracks on her face, her red nose and the puffiness beneath her closed lashes.

The letter was turned in, so Eli had no idea what it consisted of, but if he had to guess, he'd say it was something written in Todd's scratchy penmanship.

Before he could step back, Nora's eyes fluttered open and fixed on his.

"Hey," he said softly, looking down at her. "How are you feeling?"

Her gaze wasn't warm, wasn't loving like it was when he'd kissed her goodbye this morning. Something was wrong, something more than just her going through Todd's old things.

"What happened, Nora?"

She sat up, thrusting the letter toward him. "You happened. You and Todd happened, Eli," she accused, her voice husky from sleep.

His eyes skimmed over the letter to see why she was so upset, so angry. The letter was addressed to

Nora, dated only days before Todd's death...but it was the last part of the letter that Eli zeroed in on.

His knees weakened and he sat on the edge of the bed next to her.

"I don't want to hear excuses," she whispered. "There's no reason for this kind of betrayal. You said you loved me. I assumed even as a friend you would've loved me enough to tell me my husband had cheated on me."

Eli closed his eyes, as if he could possibly close out the hurt that threaded her voice. Opening his eyes, he looked back down to the damning letter in his hands.

Todd just had to go and hurt her one more time. Barely containing his rage, Eli reached up and raked his hand over his scar. He'd been so close to having her back in his life, so close to having her fill his heart like nothing else could...but because of his warped version of keeping her safe from the truth, his gentlemanly qualities blew up in his face.

Nora came to her feet, turned to look down at him. "Would you ever have told me?"

Eli met her narrowed gaze. The hurt staring back at him was like a kick to the gut. He'd never seen this side of Nora and he knew all the pain she was feeling could've somewhat been cushioned had he told her the truth in the beginning.

"No," he answered honestly. "I didn't want to cause you more pain."

On a broken sigh, she closed her eyes and rested a hand on her stomach.

Eli came to his feet. "Are you hurting?"

She laughed as she looked up at him. "You lost all rights to worry about me and this baby when you opted to lie to me. We're done, Eli."

"Nora, please, if you're in pain let me help. Think of the baby."

She brushed a strand of hair off her face. "I am thinking of my baby. I'm thinking of how I'll move forward and welcome this child into the world alone. I'm thinking of how we are done and it's time I realized that there's a reason we never worked out. I'm not in any more pain than I have been, and if I need help I'll call my actual doctor."

She'd shut him out, and he had no one to blame but himself. But he never would've told her. Ever. She didn't need to have her final memories of Todd tainted knowing he'd cheated on her. He knew she was way angrier with Eli than Todd. Eli was alive, able to disclose the truth, and yet he'd chosen to keep it to himself.

"You need to go."

Her whispered words combined with a fresh batch of tears forming in her eyes broke him. She'd erected a wall around herself and there was no way he would be able to scale it.

"No matter what you think of me," he told her, fighting the urge to touch her, to hold her, "I do love you, Nora. I love your baby and I love us. I never once lied about my feelings. If you think this through, you'll understand why I didn't tell you about Todd."

Tears spilled down her cheeks, and she didn't even

bother to swipe them away. Her chin quivered as she spoke.

"I assume it's because you two were best friends," she whispered. "Which only tells me that if you thought it was okay to keep the secret, then what's to stop you from doing it yourself?"

A pain like he'd never known sliced right through him. He swallowed through the tears clogging his own throat.

"If that's how you feel, then we don't belong together. I would never, ever cause you more hurt or purposely ruin our relationship. Love means everything to me, Nora. Our love means everything to me."

Without asking, he rested his hand on her stomach one last time before walking from the room and out of her life.

The ring in his pocket meant nothing now.

Chapter Seventeen

Thank God for the long weekend that spilled over into Christmas. The last thing Eli wanted was to come out of his apartment for Christmas dinner. He wasn't feeling too festive.

His family always celebrated on Christmas Eve, but Eli was perfectly content cozying up to his beer. Not that he had taken the first sip. He'd been sitting on his couch, holding the bottle up on the arm and staring at the label.

There were a couple of times in the army when he'd wished he were one of those guys who lost themselves for a few hours in the bottom of a bottle, but he hadn't been raised that way.

But right now, Eli would give anything to numb the pain, even if for a few minutes.

The condensation slid down the amber-colored glass and onto his fingers. Footsteps pounded up from the garage just before his apartment door flew open.

"What the hell is going on?"

Eli eyed his brother Drake across the room. Great, as if one pissy brother wasn't enough, Cameron stood just over his shoulder, too.

"Come in if you're coming in," Eli told them. "If not, go away."

"Well, you're in a mood and Nora is not speaking." Cameron stepped in, leaned against the small dinette table and crossed his arms over his chest. "What did you do?"

Eli snapped his gaze to his brother. "What makes you think I did anything?"

Drake took the time to take off his coat and toss it over the chair by the door. Cameron remained in his and shrugged, eyeing Eli.

"I'm a cop," Cam said. "I'm pretty good at reading people. She's got hurt written all over her and you're being a recluse up here at Christmas of all times, which means you're blaming yourself for something."

Eli set his full longneck on the coffee table. Resting his elbows on his knees, his head in his hands, he stared at the gray rug beneath his bare feet.

"I hurt her," Eli admitted, rubbing a hand over his bedhead. "I betrayed her trust just like Todd, and I can't blame her for not wanting to be with me."

Drake remained by the chair, hands on his hips. "Nora is down at Mom and Dad's. They insisted she come over and eat. We really didn't know anything was wrong until we saw her. She looks as if she's been crying for days, man. You've got to fix this."

Eli jerked his head up. "You don't think I want to fix this? You think I enjoy knowing I've hurt someone I love? I was ready to stay here, settle down and make a life with her. I even bought her a damn ring."

Drake and Cameron exchanged a look before Cameron crossed the room and took a seat at the end of the couch.

"I have no idea what happened, but you two can't go on like this."

"We won't," Eli stated. "I'm going to have to tell Dad I can't stay and take over his practice. I'll go back to Atlanta. I should know soon if that promotion is mine or not."

"So because you're too much of a coward to face this issue with Nora, you're leaving Dad in a bind and the only woman you've ever loved all alone?" Cameron asked. "You're a jerk."

Eli came to his feet. "Shut the hell up. You have no idea what went on. None. So don't come in here and start spewing relationship advice. What do you know, anyway? You're married to your job."

Drake came to his feet. "Calm down, Eli. You know we're both here to try to help. Do you want to tell us what happened or do you want us to leave you alone on Christmas Eve so you can cozy back up to your beer?"

Sinking back down to the couch, Eli sighed and started from the beginning. He told them about the time he'd planned on coming home for good, he told them about the affair and then he told them how he really got that scar on his face.

Eli had a feeling this wouldn't be the last time he told this story. Somehow, Nora would have to hear it. But he truly didn't think he could talk to her, not when she'd been convinced that since he kept the secret it meant he was capable of infidelity, too.

That hurt worse than anything else she'd said. She obviously didn't know him at all and everything he'd said and done to prove his love up to that point had been moot because she didn't believe it.

By the time he'd bared his soul to his brothers, it was late and he couldn't make himself go downstairs to dinner.

"Tell them I'm not feeling well. I don't care what you say, but if Nora's down there I don't want her more uncomfortable."

Cameron rolled his eyes. "You're going to have to tell her everything. And you better do it soon before this tears Mom up. She's worried about both of you."

Eli nodded. "I can't right now. I just… I can't. Okay? Tell Mom I'll be down first thing in the morning."

"Don't be surprised if Mom comes storming up here," Drake joked. "But we'll tell her."

Cameron walked out and Drake gripped the door, turning around to meet Eli's gaze across the small room. "I lost the love of my life, Eli. I can't get her back. You still have a chance to go after happiness."

And with that he was gone. Eli knew Drake lived with that hell every day of losing his fiancée in such a tragic way. He was right, though. Eli still did have a chance and maybe Nora wouldn't listen to him, but maybe she would.

Once Eli was alone again he took his beer to the small kitchen and dumped it. When he turned back around he had the strongest urge to throw something. He hadn't seen Nora for almost two days, hadn't seen her smile, hadn't tasted her lips, held her body against his...felt her baby kick.

Glancing around the small space almost depressed him more. No Christmas tree, no family, no dinner and laughter and sharing stories. But if he went down to the main house he'd only make Nora feel awkward and he'd be in a foul mood. No need in making the family dinner a miserable experience for everyone.

Besides, Nora needed family more right now. And when he returned to Atlanta, his family would continue to watch over her just like they always had. At least he had that comfort.

Damn it, he didn't want her to be watched over and cared for by his brothers and parents. He wanted to be the one she leaned on, the one who shared everything with her.

Eli went to the dinette table and booted up his laptop. Since he had nothing else to do, he went to check his work email from Atlanta. He'd been off the radar a couple of days.

And the first message he saw was the one he'd been waiting for. He'd gotten the promotion.

* * *

When Drake and Cameron had pulled her aside after dinner she'd been afraid of what they'd say. But she had no idea the bombshell they had in store.

Her nerves were on edge, her hormones were all over the place and she honestly didn't have a clue what to do next.

She rested her hands on the countertop in the galley kitchen and sighed.

"I'm making Eli a plate," Bev said, bustling into the kitchen as if she didn't know about or wasn't commenting on all the turmoil. "Would you care to run it up to him, dear?"

"Bev," Nora said, turning around. "I know you mean well, but I doubt you know what you're asking."

Setting a stack of dirty dishes on the counter, Bev crossed to Nora and took her hands in hers. "I know exactly what I'm asking," Bev said softly. "I know two people I dearly love are hurting and the only way to get past that is to talk. Communication is the key to any relationship."

Nora swallowed, praying she didn't start sobbing here. She'd been tear-free for two hours. A record for her after the past couple days.

"We don't have a relationship," Nora whispered. "I know you wanted—"

"It doesn't matter what I want or don't want," Bev interrupted. "What matters is there are two broken hearts and I can't sit back and let this happen. Now, I'm making a plate. Do you want to take it or do you want me to have Eli come down here?"

Nora closed her eyes and sighed. "I'll take it."

There was so much pain, so much anguish. The damage was too great to even get back to a friendship status—how could they ever repair what had been done?

Nora bundled herself up in her coat and scarf while Bev fixed the plate. This was the dead last thing she wanted to do, but she knew she and Eli needed to talk, no matter how much hurt lay wedged between them.

"Drake put a little salt on the walk with that fresh dusting we got, but be careful." Bev held the door open. "Take your time."

Nora knew the woman meant "take your time in the apartment," not "take your time getting *to* the apartment."

She didn't stop to think about what she was doing; she just set out toward the garage and up the steps, gripping the wooden rail for support as she went. But she did stop to knock. When he didn't answer, she tried the knob.

Nora held the plate and eased the door open. Eli sat at his small table with his back to the door.

"I told Cam and Drake to tell you I'd come down and see you and Dad tomorrow."

Nora cleared her throat. "Um… She sent me."

Eli jerked around, shooting out of his seat. And Nora froze. He'd been crying. His eyes were red, moist, and when he realized she was staring, he swiped a hand down his face.

"I'm sorry," she mumbled. "Your mom sent this up and…"

This was beyond awkward. Nora crossed to the

kitchen, purposely avoiding eye contact with Eli. She knew he would never want anyone to see him vulnerable, let alone her.

After she set the plate on the kitchen counter she turned, meeting his gaze from across the open room.

"I'm surprised you brought dinner to me," he said, his voice husky with emotion. "Thanks."

Nora nodded. "I…I needed to talk to you."

He didn't say anything, merely crossed his arms, resting his fingers along thick biceps that filled out his thin navy sweater.

"Which brother got ahold of you?" he asked.

He had to have known when he spilled the full truth to his siblings that one of them would rush to tell her.

"It doesn't matter which one, Eli. The point is you didn't tell me everything."

His eyes raked over her, then he shook his head. "Might as well take off your coat."

Nora unbuttoned her coat and laid it and her scarf over the back of the chair by the door. Tugging her shirt down to cover her bump, she crossed the room and took a seat on the sofa.

When he came closer she couldn't help but look right at the scar. That was the part Cam and Drake had refused to tell her about. They both told her to ask Eli, but they did tell her enough to know that it would possibly change her mind.

"What all did you hear?" he asked as he stayed still by the table.

"Your brothers defending you," she told him.

"They were plenty mad at you, but they believed you had a good reason for keeping something so monumental from me."

Eli nodded. "And what do you think?"

"That I want to hear your reasons. They seem to think I'll be surprised at your side of the story."

Eli's brows rose. "The other day it didn't matter. You even went so far as to practically accuse me of thinking infidelity was okay."

Nora looked down at her clasped hands over her belly. "I'm sorry, Eli. I didn't know what to think. To be honest, I still don't."

When she looked back up to him and saw his jaw clenching, she knew she wasn't going anywhere anytime soon. Now that they'd both had time to let everything settle, they had so much to discuss.

"My husband is gone, Eli," she went on. "But even when he was here, he was gone. Nothing about his missions was discussed. He never wanted to let me into that part of his life. And not only did he die, he'd sent me divorce papers while I was carrying his child. To top off all of that, I find out he'd been unfaithful and you knew about it. How could I not be angry? You were always the one person I could count on, Eli."

Anger started bubbling in her the more she talked. Unable to remain seated, she got back up and started crossing the room as she spoke.

"No matter what happened years ago, you were always the one person I swore would always be honest. You were always the one to do the right thing in the end."

"The right thing?" he demanded, staring down at her. "I tried doing the right thing years ago, Nora. I got out of the army with intentions of going to medical school and coming home to be with you. I wanted to see if we could have a life together."

Nora gasped. "I never knew this," she whispered.

"Yeah, that's because when I got done with school, you and Todd were engaged. What the hell could I do at that point but watch my best friend and the love of my life live happily ever after? Only I couldn't stay here. So I reenlisted."

Nora gripped the back of one of the chairs at the table. She needed stability because she had a feeling he wasn't done pouring out all of his emotions.

"But then I had to hear Todd talk about the two of you," he went on. "At first he discussed the wedded bliss and how lucky he was. Then he started wondering if you two rushed into marriage and toward the end he knew you two had made a mistake and he was afraid to hurt you."

"For a man who was afraid to hurt me, he sure did do a lot on purpose to do just that."

Eli nodded. "We were at a bar one night when we were overseas. We had both drank way too much. He disappeared for a while and when he came back with a woman, I knew. I just knew."

Nora steeled herself for the details she wasn't sure she was ready to hear. But she needed to know, needed to hear what Eli had to say.

"We got into a fight," Eli went on. "I told him he wasn't worthy of you and he told me that he knew he'd never measure up to me where you were concerned. He kept saying over and over that I should've married you, that you never looked at him the way you did me."

Nora's eyes darted to the scar.

"Yeah, that was from the fight." Eli muttered a curse. "We tore that bar up fighting and my face met the glass on a mirror."

Over her. Nora couldn't imagine the fact that halfway around the world those two men had been fighting over her.

"I told him if he didn't come clean with you, then I would." Eli raked his hands through his hair and met her gaze. "I hated the thought of you being hurt, Nora, but I also knew you deserved to know. He swore he'd tell you, and when he came home on leave I assumed he was going to. By the time he came back, my tour was nearly up and he told me not to say anything. That he was writing you a letter because he couldn't do it face-to-face."

Nora bit her lip, trying to keep her emotions under control.

"I honestly had no idea about the divorce papers," he whispered. "I swear to you."

A tear slipped down his cheek. The image of this big strong man, a man who'd fought in a war, a man who cared for wounded and dying, was crying…for her, for them.

"I've decided to leave at the end of dad's medical leave," he went on, swiping the tear as if it meant nothing. "There's a job I've been waiting to hear on in Atlanta and I just found out I got it."

The very last thread of hope in Nora died. She hadn't even realized she'd come here with the minuscule light left in her heart, but now that it had been doused with his words, she felt even more empty than before.

"Um… That's great," she told him. "Congratulations."

He nodded, his eyes not quite meeting hers. "Thanks."

She stared at him, waiting for him to say something, to say he was joking and he didn't mean to hurt her…anything. He remained silent.

Nora wrung her hands together before turning toward the chair by the door to get her coat. She needed to get out of here, needed distance and needed to realize that her life with Eli was officially over. There was no third chance and this second chance had been blown to pieces so small only slivers remained.

Just as she reached for her scarf, Eli's strong hands gripped her shoulders.

"Fight for us, damn it." His words were thick with emotion and she knew if she turned she'd see those tears back in his eyes. "If this is what you want, fight."

Nora dropped her head into her hands and sobbed as Eli pulled her back against his hard chest. His hands came around to rest on her stomach.

"I know I hurt you, Nora. I know you feel betrayed, but I swear on my life, I did it out of love." His fingers spread over her belly as the baby started moving. "But you hurt me, too, when you said I was capable of infidelity. You know, deep down, that I'm not. I could never even look at another woman when you are all that I've ever wanted."

Along with the warmth of being surrounded by Eli's powerful touch, his words fueled her with a promise that maybe this second chance wasn't dead. Maybe they both had to fight.

"I don't think you'd be unfaithful," she whispered between sniffs. "I was hurting so bad I wanted you to hurt, too."

"I love you." He took her shoulders and turned her around. Sure enough, tears swam in his eyes. "There's no fancy way to say it. I love you because I want to give everything to you. I want to take care of you. Love isn't about what you get in return, but what you give, and there was no way I was going to give you more heartache than you'd already experienced."

He was wrong—there was a fancy way to say I love you and he'd just delivered it in a nicely wrapped package.

Nora's fingertips trailed over the scar. "You let everyone think you got this overseas."

"I did."

Hand hovering over his face, she smiled. "But you got it because of me."

Taking her hand, he kissed her palm and laid it back over the scar. "And I'd do it all again. I'd fight for you every day of my life, Nora. You can't possibly know the love I feel for you. You can't even fathom how my heart was so empty when I was away from you for all those years because I can't even find words to describe it."

"I know exactly how you're feeling." She framed his face with her hands, wiping the tears that had slid down his stubbled cheeks. "I don't want to live without you, Eli. And if that means I need to move to Atlanta, then I will. Wherever you want to go, I'll go. Are you sure you're up to taking me and this baby? We're a team and not many men would want to raise another man's child."

Eli's hands slid down to cover her belly again. "Regardless of how Todd and I left things before he died, I loved him like one of my brothers. Raising his baby, your baby, is not even an issue with me. I'll love this baby like my own and treat her as such. She'll never question where I stand."

He nipped at her lips and rested his forehead against hers. "And neither will you."

Eli's mouth covered hers once again, hotter and hungrier than before. She wrapped her arms around his neck and leaned into him as his hands traveled down to cup her behind.

"I want you," he muttered against her lips. "What did the doctor say?"

"I've been given the green light for all activity." Already her body started responding to his touch, his whispered declaration. "I'm healthy and so is my baby girl."

When he scooped her up and started toward his bed, Nora laughed. "Your mother is going to know what we're doing if I don't come back down."

"She'll be thrilled when you don't come back down because she wants you in this family just as much as I do."

Eli sat Nora down on the edge of the bed. "Don't move."

Confused, she watched as he raced to the drawer in the coffee table and took out a small box. A velvet box.

Nora's breath caught in her throat as he came back and knelt before her.

"Eli—"

"I know it's soon," he said, cutting her off. "But hear me out. I'm not asking you to marry me. Yet. But I am asking you to wear my ring. I don't care how long we're engaged, I don't care how long you need to get over Todd, to get past all this hurt. I will be here, Nora."

She stared as he lifted the lid and a thick band of diamonds stared back at her.

"I wanted to keep the ring flat so you could still wear it to work and not scratch the baby." He removed it from the box and she saw diamonds all the way around the band with a platinum setting. "Please say you'll wear it."

Her eyes met his as she smiled. "Of course I'll wear it, Eli. And I don't need to wait. I'll marry you tomorrow if you want."

He chuckled as he slid the ring in place. "Tomorrow is Christmas, honey."

"Then the next day. I'll marry you anytime."

Leaning up, Eli kissed her softly. "We'll marry

soon, but my mother will want to make it a big deal because she never thought any of us St. John boys would actually settle down."

"Oh, my gosh. I keep forgetting. I want to throw your parents a surprise anniversary party." Nora studied his face. "What do you think? I've been meaning to ask since you came home, but…well, you kept sidetracking me."

He nipped at her lips once more. "I think it's a great idea. And, honey, you're the one who sidetracked *me*."

Nora stared down at the ring, loving how he'd taken such care in choosing one for her lifestyle and taken her baby into consideration.

"I don't want to go to Atlanta," he told her. "I want to stay here with you and run Dad's practice."

Her baby kicked, as if approving of that plan. "I think that's the best idea I've heard," she told him, looping her arms back around his neck and tugging him up onto the bed.

"I hope you don't mind if your dinner is cold," she muttered against his lips. "Because I plan on keeping you here for a while."

His hands traveled up under her shirt. "Keep me here as long as you want. I'm yours forever."

Forever. All she'd ever wanted wrapped in one simple word.

* * * * *

COMING NEXT MONTH FROM

HARLEQUIN®

SPECIAL EDITION

Available November 18, 2014

#2371 THE CHRISTMAS RANCH

The Cowboys of Cold Creek • by RaeAnne Thayne

Hope Nichols hadn't found her passion in life...until now. When her relatives decide to shut down the holiday attraction at their Christmas Ranch, Hope leaps into action. She works to make this Christmas the best ever with the help of hunky Rafe Santiago. The former navy SEAL is drawn to the lovely Hope, but a long-buried secret threatens to destroy their burgeoning relationship...

#2372 A BRAVO CHRISTMAS WEDDING

The Bravo Royales • by Christine Rimmer

Aurora Bravo-Calabretti, princess of Montedoro, is used to the best of everything—including men. So when her crush, mountain man Walker McKellan, becomes her bodyguard, Rory is determined to make him hers. There's just one catch—Walker doesn't believe he's right for Rory. Can royal Rory make the Colorado cowboy hers in time for Christmas?

#2373 A ROYAL CHRISTMAS PROPOSAL

Royal Babies • by Leanne Banks

It's Christmastime in Chantaine, and Princess Fredericka Deveraux has returned home with her hearing-disabled son, Leo. When her brother insists that Ericka needs a bodyguard, she disagrees...until she sees her new employee. Former football player Treat Walker is a treat for the eyes—but the princess and her protector both agree they can't act on their mutual attraction. That is, until Santa works his magic under the mistletoe!

#2374 A VERY MAVERICK CHRISTMAS

Montana Mavericks: 20 Years in the Saddle! • by Rachel Lee

Who's that girl? is the question on the lips of everyone in Rust Creek Falls this holiday season. Julie Smith is searching for the answer to that very question. She doesn't know her real name or anything about herself—just that she might discover more in Rust Creek Falls. Local cowboy Braden Traub is drawn to Julie and tries to help her find the key to this puzzle. Can the amnesiac and the maverick solve the mystery of her past in time to create a future together?

#2375 THE LAWMAN'S NOELLE

Men of the West • by Stella Bagwell

Ranch owner Noelle Barnes doesn't need a man—least of all one who's both a handsome member of the wealthy Calhoun clan *and* a lawman. But Evan Calhoun isn't like anyone else she's ever met. For one, he's irresistibly charming. Besides, he wants to use his abilities to do good in their community. As Noelle and Evan's initial disagreements turn into long, sultry nights, the sparks between them might just turn into the fire of love.

#2376 A TEXAS RESCUE CHRISTMAS

Texas Rescue • by Caro Carson

Two outcasts find love as Christmas hits Texas. Former college football player Trey Waterson once suffered a career-ending head injury that impaired some of his cognitive functions. Frustrated, Trey desperately wants to prove himself. His chance comes with heiress Becky Cargill, who's fleeing her malicious mother. When Trey saves Becky's life, sparks fly. But can they move beyond their tragic pasts to find forever together?

YOU CAN FIND MORE INFORMATION ON UPCOMING HARLEQUIN® TITLES, FREE EXCERPTS AND MORE AT WWW.HARLEQUIN.COM.

HSECNM1114

REQUEST YOUR FREE BOOKS!
2 FREE NOVELS PLUS 2 FREE GIFTS!

⬢ HARLEQUIN®

SPECIAL EDITION
Life, Love & Family

YES! Please send me 2 FREE Harlequin® Special Edition novels and my 2 FREE gifts (gifts are worth about $10). After receiving them, if I don't wish to receive any more books, I can return the shipping statement marked "cancel." If I don't cancel, I will receive 6 brand-new novels every month and be billed just $4.74 per book in the U.S. or $5.24 per book in Canada. That's a savings of at least 14% off the cover price! It's quite a bargain! Shipping and handling is just 50¢ per book in the U.S. and 75¢ per book in Canada.* I understand that accepting the 2 free books and gifts places me under no obligation to buy anything. I can always return a shipment and cancel at any time. Even if I never buy another book, the two free books and gifts are mine to keep forever.

235/335 HDN F45Y

Name _____ (PLEASE PRINT) _____

Address _____ Apt. # _____

City _____ State/Prov. _____ Zip/Postal Code _____

Signature (if under 18, a parent or guardian must sign)

Mail to the **Harlequin® Reader Service:**
IN U.S.A.: P.O. Box 1867, Buffalo, NY 14240-1867
IN CANADA: P.O. Box 609, Fort Erie, Ontario L2A 5X3

Want to try two free books from another line?
Call 1-800-873-8635 or visit www.ReaderService.com.

* Terms and prices subject to change without notice. Prices do not include applicable taxes. Sales tax applicable in N.Y. Canadian residents will be charged applicable taxes. Offer not valid in Quebec. This offer is limited to one order per household. Not valid for current subscribers to Harlequin Special Edition books. All orders subject to credit approval. Credit or debit balances in a customer's account(s) may be offset by any other outstanding balance owed by or to the customer. Please allow 4 to 6 weeks for delivery. Offer available while quantities last.

Your Privacy—The Harlequin® Reader Service is committed to protecting your privacy. Our Privacy Policy is available online at www.ReaderService.com or upon request from the Harlequin Reader Service.

We make a portion of our mailing list available to reputable third parties that offer products we believe may interest you. If you prefer that we not exchange your name with third parties, or if you wish to clarify or modify your communication preferences, please visit us at www.ReaderService.com/consumerschoice or write to us at Harlequin Reader Service Preference Service, P.O. Box 9062, Buffalo, NY 14269. Include your complete name and address.

HSE13R

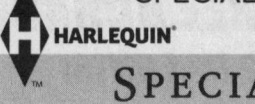
***

The whole time he worked, he was aware of her—the pure blue of her eyes, her skin, dusted with pink from the cold, the soft curves as she reached over her head to hand him the end of the light string.

"That should do it for me," he said after a moment. In more ways than one.

"Good work. Should we plug them in so we can see how they look?"

"Sure."

She went inside the little structure at the entrance to the village, where she must have flipped a few switches. They had finished only about half, but the cottages with lights indeed looked magical against the pearly twilight spreading across the landscape as the sun set.

"Ahhh. Beautiful," she exclaimed. "I never get tired of that."

"Truly lovely," he agreed, though he was looking at her and not the cottages.

She smiled at him. "I'm sorry you gave up your whole afternoon to help me, but the truth is I would have been sunk without you. Thank you."

"You're welcome. I can finish these up when I get here in the morning, after I take Joey to school. Now that I've sort of figured out what I'm doing, I should be able to get these lights hung in no time and start work on the repairs at the Lodge by midmorning."

She smiled at him again, a bright, vibrant smile that made his heart pound as if he had just raced up to the top of those mountains up there and back.

"You are the best Christmas present ever, Rafe. Seriously."

He raised an eyebrow. "Am I?"

He didn't mean the words to sound like innuendo but he was almost certain that sudden flush on her cheeks had nothing to do with the cool November air.

"You know what I mean."

He did. She was talking about his help around the ranch. He was taken by surprise by a sudden fierce longing that her words should mean something completely different.

"I'm not sure I've ever been anyone's favorite Christmas gift before," he murmured.

She gave him a sidelong look. "Then it's about time, isn't it?"

***

Hope Nichols was never able to find her place in the world—until her family's Colorado holiday attraction, the Christmas Ranch, faces closure. This Christmas, she's determined to rescue the ranch with the help of handsome former Navy SEAL Rafe Santiago and his adorable nephew. As sparks fly between mysterious Rafe and Hope, this Christmas will be one that nobody in Cold Creek will ever forget!

Don't miss THE CHRISTMAS RANCH
available December 2014, wherever
Harlequin® Special Edition books and ebooks are sold!

Coming in December 2014

A BRAVO CHRISTMAS WEDDING

by *New York Times* bestselling author

Christine Rimmer

Aurora Bravo-Calabretti, princess of Montedoro, is used to the best of everything—including men. So when her crush, mountain man Walker McKellan, becomes her bodyguard, Rory is determined to make him hers. There's just one catch—Walker doesn't believe he's right for Rory. Can royal Rory make the Colorado cowboy hers in time for Christmas?

Don't miss the latest edition of
***THE BRAVO ROYALES** miniseries!*

Available wherever books and ebooks are sold!